CLASS ASSEMBLIES 2

Ready-to-use assemblies for whole-class performances

Veronica Clark

Kaye Umansky

Jenny McLachlan

Contents

Introduction 3-4

Precious to Me 5-14
   Script 6-12
   Teaching Notes 13-14

Tiddalik 15-26
   Script 16-22
   Teaching Notes 23-26

Monsters Ps and Qs 27-36
   Script 28-33
   Teaching Notes 34-36

The Mirror of Truth 37-49
   Script 38-45
   Teaching Notes 46-49

Stage Plans 50-52
SEAL Links 53-55

Melody Lines 56-63

Performance licence information 64
About the authors 64
Acknowledgements 64

Introduction

Class Assemblies 2 contains everything you need to put on a successful class performance; perfect for whole-class assemblies or an end of term production for a wider audience.

The book contains:
- scripts/stories
- curriculum-based activities
- links to SEAL and literacy units
- performance tips
- melody lines for the songs

The CD contains:
- sung performances and backing tracks to sing along with
- incidental music to use in your performance (including entry and exit music for each assembly)

Whatever your resources, and whether you are aiming for something large scale, or simple and basic, this book will help you to stage a successful performance. The title page of each story provides a quick overview of the cast, story, theme and songs, and the performance notes and stage plans supply further ideas for rehearsing and staging the assembly stories.

The assemblies aim to be as flexible as possible. Although the four plays are designed for a specific age group, they can be adapted for use with other age groups.

You could present the plays as stories for use in the classroom to prompt discussion. The *Literacy Links* boxes show where you could incorporate the stories into literacy work. Each play is based around a simple moral or message, which is explored in the PSHE notes in the *Curriculum Links* section and outlined on the title page.

Preparing for the assembly

Familiarise the children with the play by reading it through a couple of times, like a story, and then discuss it with the class (see PSHE notes and *SEAL Links*). Work through some of the activities in the *Curriculum Links*. Involve the children in collecting and making props and costumes.

Take the opportunity to introduce children to new vocabulary, for example, **cast**, **props**, **scenery**, **scripts**.

Casting

Numbers for various parts are approximate, and are based on an average class size of 30. Adapt to suit your class. Some of the parts involve the children remembering lines. Make sure that the children are familiar with the cues to their lines in the narration, and encourage them to project their voices and avoid turning away from the audience when they are speaking or singing. Discuss the characters the children are playing and help them to give a convincing performance. If children have trouble remembering their lines, consider attaching their text to a prop, or incorporate some of the lines into the narration.

Staging and performance tips

Adapt these to suit your needs. You can ignore, embellish, adapt or simplify them.

Stage directions such as **stage back left** or **stage front right** are interpreted by imagining you are standing on the stage facing the audience (see also *Stage Plans*).

The stage plans show starting positions, where to put props and scenery, and the movement around the stage area.

Venue and acting space

The notes assume the plays are being performed in a large room, such as a hall. Adapt to your circumstances.

The word **stage** refers to the main performance area. This can either be a designated area of floor space or a raised stage. Teachers using a raised stage will need between one and three sets of steps for movement on and off the stage.

References to **off stage** and **below the stage** describe space outside the main performance area. Where a raised stage is being used, they refer to activity at floor level.

The stage plans

The stage plans at the back of the book are drawn on squared backgrounds. Each square represents one square metre. Adapt the plans to suit your needs.

It may sometimes be helpful to use tape or chalk to show children where to stand and the routes they take.

Costumes

Costume suggestions are given in the performance notes. For a smaller-scale production, simplify the costumes, or consider using only one element, eg, headdresses. Adding noses, whiskers, spots, etc, using face paints, can add an exciting dimension to performances.

Storytellers (narrators)

Adults can perform all the narration, or, as indicated in some of the scripts, the storyteller's part can be split between children. Make sure the narrators are visible by standing them on stage blocks or PE benches. Spoken lines written for individual children can be incorporated into the storyteller's part. If possible, use microphones for storytellers. Consider giving them something special to wear, even if it's only best clothes, or bow ties and shirts.

Songs and chants

The songs in this pack are catchy and easy to learn: some consist of new words to well-known tunes, and some are simple original songs.

Sound effects

A group of children could be chosen to make any necessary sound effects. If you do so, reduce the number of cast members without speaking parts.

Precious to Me by Jenny McLachlan

Cast

Lead storyteller
Ben's storyteller
Grace's storyteller
Nafisa's storyteller
Freddie's storyteller
Mr (Miss, Mrs) Richards
Ben

Grace (dancer)
Nafisa (guitarist)
Freddie and Kabir (karate enthusiasts)
Alex, Heather, Craig and Joe (ask questions at end)
The rest of Ben's classmates (about 13)
Ben's dad
Ben's mum

Ben and his teacher, Mr Richards, have quite big parts to learn, but the rest of the named characters have only one or two lines. The teacher's part could be played by a child or an adult.

Assembly theme

This story encourages children to reflect on things that are important in life, and emphasises that the things that are most precious to us often don't cost much money.

Story

Ben's teacher has introduced a show-and-tell session with a difference. He asks his pupils to bring something that is special to them into school.

Grace has been to Spain, and has brought back a pair of castanets. She invites a few friends to join her in an improvised Spanish dance. Nafisa has been given an electric guitar and amplifier for her birthday, and she and a few others form a class band. And there's Freddie, with his yellow karate belt. He, Kabir, and a few other pupils demonstrate their balancing skills.

Ben can't decide what to bring in. Nothing he owns is as impressive as his classmates' precious objects. But, at the last minute, Ben has an inspiration. He remembers something extremely special to him. It is only when his mum appears, holding his baby sister, that Mr Richards and his classmates find out what is the most important thing in the world to Ben.

Setting

Most of the story takes place in a classroom, although there are three short scenes at Ben's house.

Songs

I wonder and *Holidays* have original tunes. The remaining songs have familiar melodies. *Let our music come alive* is used to demonstrate Nafisa's guitar-playing.

Script: Precious to Me

Scene 1: Grace's castanets

LEAD STORYTELLER

It was nearly the end of the school day, and Ben was sitting quietly on the carpet with the rest of his class.

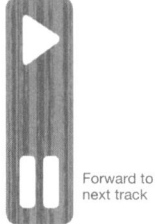
Forward to next track

SONG: I WONDER *(Original)*

The world is full of wonders and delights,
Like friends and pets and toys and frosty nights.
But if I had to choose something precious to me,
I wonder what that special thing would be?

GRACE'S STORYTELLER:

Grace Simmonds was standing next to Mr Richards, clicking and clacking a pair of shiny castanets.

MR RICHARDS

Grace has brought some castanets to show us today. Why are the castanets precious to you, Grace?

GRACE

They remind me of when I went to Spain with my dad.

MR RICHARDS

Can you show us how it's done?

GRACE'S STORYTELLER

Grace picked some friends to join her in the middle of the carpet, and they did a twirling dance while Grace clicked her castanets.

(ACTION – GRACE AND HER FRIENDS STAND UP AND DANCE TO *HOLIDAYS*.)

Forward to next track

SONG: HOLIDAYS *(Original)*

Holidays are precious times,
When everything feels good and new.
Blue skies and special treats,
Laughter and friendships too.

LEAD STORYTELLER

The children in Mr Richard's class were taking it in turns to bring something that was precious to them into school, and to talk about it. Mr Richards was working through the alphabet. Yasmin Adams had been the first, and Ben would be the last, because his surname was Yaafe. Ben was dreading his day, because he couldn't think of anything precious to bring in.

Scene 2: Ben's stick of rock

(ACTION – BEN WALKS OVER TO HIS HOUSE.)

BEN'S STORYTELLER

That evening, Ben was playing football with his dad in the living room.

(ACTION – BEN KICKS A SOFT BABY BALL AROUND.)

Well, his dad wasn't really playing, he was holding Ben's baby sister, Isobel, at the same time.

(ACTION – DAD ROCKS ISOBEL.)

BEN

Dad, can we go on holiday to Spain?

DAD

Not this year, Ben. We can't afford it.

BEN'S STORYTELLER

The last time they went on holiday was to Ben's Nan's in Eastbourne. Ben still had half a piece of Eastbourne rock that had gone soft, but he couldn't take that into school as his precious object!

 **REPEAT SONG: I WONDER**

The world is full of wonders and delights ...

Forward to next track

(ACTION – GROUP OF CHILDREN HOLD UP A LARGE MODEL OR PICTURE OF A PIECE OF ROCK. THE CHILDREN SHAKE THEIR HEADS.)

Scene 3: Nafisa's guitar

(ACTION – BEN RETURNS TO THE CLASSROOM.)

NAFISA'S STORYTELLER
Now it was Nafisa's turn. She stood next to Mr Richards, holding an electric guitar plugged into an amplifier.

MR RICHARDS
Nafisa has brought her guitar to show us today. Why is the guitar precious to you, Nafisa?

NAFISA
I got this for my birthday and now I'm having lessons.

NAFISA'S STORYTELLER
And then she played a few chords.

(ACTION – NAFISA PLAYS SOME CHORDS ON THE GUITAR, OR MIMES.)

The sound came crashing out of the amp and everyone gasped. Nafisa looked like a real pop star.

MR RICHARDS
Let's see if we can form a rock band!

NAFISA'S STORYTELLER
Nafisa chose some children to pick an instrument from the music trolley. They stood with Nafisa and performed for the class.

(ACTION – NAFISA POINTS OUT TWO OR THREE FRIENDS, WHO CHOOSE INSTRUMENTS FROM A BOX AND STAND AT THE FRONT. THE REST OF THE CHILDREN STAND AND SING.)

Forward to next track

CD 5/14

SONG: LET OUR MUSIC COME ALIVE *(Once I caught a fish alive)*

One, two, three, four, five,
Let our music come alive.
Six, seven, eight, nine, ten,
Hit those joyful notes again.

Script – PRECIOUS TO ME

Scene 4: Ben's keyboard

(ACTION – BEN WALKS OVER TO HIS HOUSE.)

BEN'S STORYTELLER
Later that evening, Ben's mum was getting tea ready, while Ben rocked Isobel in her cot. Isobel was gurgling away to herself.

BEN
Mum, can I have guitar lessons?

(ACTION – BEN'S MUM SHAKES HER HEAD.)

MUM
Sorry Ben. Why don't you play your keyboard?

LEAD STORYTELLER
Ben's keyboard was ancient. His dad had found it at a car boot fair and half of the sounds didn't work. He couldn't take that in to school; everyone would laugh at him. What could he take into school as his precious object?

CD 6/15

▶
⏸ Forward to next track

REPEAT SONG: I WONDER

The world is full of wonders and delights ...

(ACTION – GROUP OF CHILDREN HOLD UP A MODEL OR PICTURE OF A BROKEN KEYBOARD. CHILDREN SHAKE THEIR HEADS.)

Scene 5: Freddie's karate belt

(ACTION – BEN RETURNS TO SCHOOL.)

FREDDIE'S STORYTELLER
Thursday was Freddie's turn. He stood next to Mr Richards, clutching a plastic bag.

MR RICHARDS
What precious object have you got in there, Freddie?

FREDDIE
It's my yellow karate belt.

MR RICHARDS
Don't practise your karate chops on me!

KABIR

Karate lessons aren't about fighting. They teach you to work as a team, and they improve your balance.

FREDDIE'S STORYTELLER

Mr Richards chose a group of children to do some balancing exercises with Freddie. They all stood at the front of the class, wobbling around on one leg.

(ACTION – THE CLASS STAND. EVERYONE BALANCES ON ONE LEG.)

No one was as good as Freddie and Kabir. They both balanced as still and as straight as storks.

SONG: **WIBBLE WOBBLE** (*Jelly on a plate*)

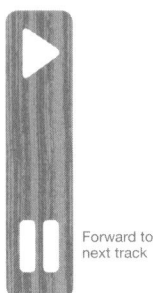

Forward to next track

**Balance on one leg,
Balance on one leg.
Wibble wobble,
Steady steady,
Balance on one leg.**

BEN'S STORYTELLER

As Ben watched Freddie showing the class how to balance, he felt really worried. He didn't go to any sports clubs. He did have a good leather football, but it was all battered and deflated. What precious object could he bring in?

REPEAT SONG: **I WONDER**

Forward to next track

The world is full of wonders and delights ...

(ACTION – GROUP OF CHILDREN HOLD UP A MODEL OR PICTURE OF A DEFLATED FOOTBALL. CHILDREN SHAKE THEIR HEADS.)

LEAD STORYTELLER

At the end of the day, Mr Richards called Ben over.

MR RICHARDS

It's your turn tomorrow, Ben. Have you got your precious object ready to show the class?

LEAD STORYTELLER

Ben didn't know what to say ... but then, he had an idea!

He remembered something precious that he had and he knew that no one else in the class, or even in the world, had one just like his. He wasn't sure if he would be able to get it into school. He would have to ask his mum.

BEN

Errr … can it be a surprise?

MR RICHARDS

Yes – that will be a great end to the week!

Scene 6: Ben's special surprise

BEN'S STORYTELLER

The next day, at 2.30, Mr Richards called Ben to the front of the class.

(ACTION – BEN GOES TO STAND BY MR RICHARDS.)

Everyone was sitting on the carpet looking up at him, waiting to hear what his precious object was.

MR RICHARDS

So where's this mystery object, Ben?

BEN

It'll be here in a minute.

MR RICHARDS

Let's try to guess what it is. You can ask Ben questions that can only be answered 'yes' or 'no'.

ALEX

Is it big? It must be if your mum has to bring it.

(ACTION – BEN SHAKES HIS HEAD.)

HEATHER

Does it weigh more than me?

(ACTION – BEN SHAKES HIS HEAD.)

CRAIG

Does it move?

(ACTION – BEN NODS.)

JOE
Does it use batteries?

(ACTION – BEN SHAKES HIS HEAD, SMILING.)

JENNIFER
Does it make a noise?

(ACTION – BEN NODS VIGOROUSLY.)

BEN'S STORYTELLER
Before they could ask any more questions, there was a knock at the classroom door, and Ben's mum and dad came in. Ben's mum was carrying his baby sister wrapped in a blanket.

BEN
My precious object is my baby sister, Isobel.

(ACTION – MR RICHARDS OFFERS HIS CHAIR TO BEN'S MUM. BEN'S DAD STANDS BEHIND HER. MR RICHARDS MOVES TO THE BACK OF THE CLASS. BEN KNEELS ON THE FLOOR AND ENTERTAINS THE BABY.)

BEN'S STORYTELLER
Just then, Isobel started crying, and Ben demonstrated all the things he could do to make Isobel laugh, like playing peep-bo, making things fall off his head and pulling funny faces. The rest of the class joined in.

(ACTION – CLASS PULL FACES AT THE BABY.)

Then Ben held Isobel. As he rocked her gently, she quickly settled down and fell asleep.

(ACTION – BEN PICKS UP HIS SISTER AND ROCKS HER IN HIS ARMS.)

MR RICHARDS
Well, I think we know who's precious to Isobel, don't we, class?

(ACTION – EVERYONE NODS AND BEN GIVES A HUGE GRIN. THE CLASS STANDS UP FOR THE FINAL SONG.)

 **REPEAT SONG: I WONDER**

The world is full of wonders and delights ...

  Script – PRECIOUS TO ME

Performance Notes

Staging and performance tips (see stage plan)

- Most of the action takes place in a classroom (the main stage area). On three occasions we visit Ben's house (in front of the stage). Mr Richards sits front right. His pupils (approximately 22 children) sit in two large semi-circular rows on the floor, around the back and left of the stage. During the classroom scenes, Ben's mum and dad wait off-stage right.

- **Scene 1**: Grace Simmonds stands facing Mr Richards. During the dance, the children not involved in the dancing mime castanet playing.

- **Scene 2**: Ben leaves the stage by the classroom door and meets up with his dad, who walks on from the right. They kick a soft ball around the front of the main stage.

- **Scene 3**: Nafsia can mime to *Let our music come alive*, or play along with it. While the instruments are put away, Ben leaves the stage and joins his mum and sister in front of the stage in the middle.

- **Scene 5**: Freddie and Kabir balance firmly, but everyone else wobbles.

- **Scene 6**: Ben should exaggerate his nods and shakes for the benefit of the audience.

Scenery

- Attach samples of the children's work to a display board and place at the back left hand side of the stage.

Props

- Spanish-style castanets.
- Electric guitar and amplifier.
- Box of school percussion instruments.
- Life-size baby doll and rocking crib.
- Soft ball (baby toy).
- Large model or picture of a stick of rock, battered football and tatty keyboard.

Costumes

- The pupils wear what they usually wear to school.

☼Curriculum Links

☼ PSHE

- Invite children to bring in holiday souvenirs (like Grace's castanets) that have a special significance. Then have a session looking at favourite gifts (like Nafisa's guitar). Finally, make a collection of special things linked to hobbies (like Freddie's yellow karate belt). Ask the children to explain in a few words why these items are precious to them.

ACTIVITY BOX: BEYOND PRICE
Invite the children to think and talk about things that are special to them that can't be bought. They could consider old things that have belonged to other people, things they have found, or memories of things they have seen, heard or smelt.

Ben's worries
- Ask the children why Ben worried so much about what to bring into school to show his classmates. Is anyone in the class a worrier like Ben? Does worrying make things better?

☼ Music

- Enquire at a local secondary school to see if they have a student band that would come into school and perform for the children. Identify the various instruments, and ask the musicians to explain how they produce their instrumental sounds. Do they pluck, strum, blow or tap? How do they make sounds go higher and lower, louder and quieter? Prior to the visit, help the children to prepare questions to ask the musicians, eg, 'Why did you learn to play the drums?' 'Where do you have lessons?' 'Do you write your own music?' 'Who are your favourite bands?'

☼ Art and Design Technology

- Make drawings of an electric guitar and label the key parts.

- Design and make drums out of tins, boxes and tubes. Use in music sessions. Have a go at making suspended cymbals. Make hard and soft beaters. Pastry brushes and nylon bottle brushes produce interesting effects.

Tiddalik by Kaye Umansky

Cast

Storyteller (adult)	Kangaroo
Tiddalik, the frog	Wombat (tells a joke)
Eel	Emu (tells a joke)
Possum	Koala (tells a joke)
Crocodile	Other Australian animals – any of the
Scorpion	above (about 10)
Kookaburra	River, billabong and lake dancers
Frog chorus (optional)	(about 9)

If preferred, lines in bold, upper case can be spoken by all the children rather than just one actor.

Assembly theme

The Aboriginal story of Tiddalik illustrates that humour can be more persuasive than force, and considers the importance of sharing limited resources.

Story

Long, long ago, in the Dreaming, it rains and rains. The dry billabongs, lakes and riverbeds fill up with water. Tiddalik the frog wakes up with a great thirst and, despite the pleas of the other animals, drinks every last drop of water in the land. The animals are furious and gather round Tiddalik, threatening to attack him. Tiddalik is terrified, but is so full of water that he can't run away – he can't even talk!

Eel comes up with a surprising suggestion: 'Why don't we try to make him laugh?' The animals tell jokes and pull funny faces, but Tiddalik's mouth stays firmly shut ... so Eel offers to perform his famous *Eel dance*.

Everyone joins in, and the floor is a mass of wriggling, twisting animals. Tiddalik's mouth twitches, then he smiles, giggles, and finally laughs. Water gushes out of his mouth, and the billabongs, lakes and rivers fill up again.

Setting

The story is set in the Australian bush, and features a billabong, a lake and a river.

Songs, chants and dances

The first song is set to a familiar tune, and the other two have new, catchy melodies. The frog chorus could sing *Thirsty*. The play opens with a rain dance. The *Eel dance* comes towards the end of the play.

Script: Tiddalik

Scene 1: A Great, Big Thirst

Long, long ago, in the Dreaming, after a long drought – it finally rained.

MUSIC: RAIN DANCE (*Original*)

Forward to
next track

The rain filled the river, the billabong and the lake. The animals swam and fished and drank their fill. There was enough water for everyone.
(ACTION – THE ANIMALS PLAY IN THE WATER.)

But then ... a bad thing happened. A frog called Tiddalik woke up with a Great Big Thirst. My, how thirsty he was. No frog had ever been that thirsty.
(ACTION – TIDDALIK WAKES.)

SONG: THIRSTY (*What shall we do with the drunken sailor?*)

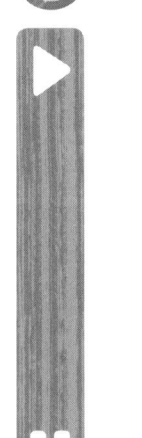

Forward to
next track

Pardon me do if I have a moan,
My mouth's as dry as a dingo's bone,
This thirst is the worst that I've ever known,
Tiddalik is thirsty!

Water! I am gasping!
Water! Throat is rasping!
Water! Must have water,
Tiddalik is thirsty!

He looked all about him for something to drink.
(ACTION – TIDDALIK LOOKS AROUND.)

Something cool. Something soothing. Something wet. And his eye caught the gleaming river. He said:

HMMM. I'LL HAVE THAT!

Down he went to the river.
(ACTION – TIDDALIK WADDLES DOWN TO THE RIVER.)

All the animals saw him coming. They cried:

SONG: NO*! NO!* (*What shall we do with the drunken sailor*)

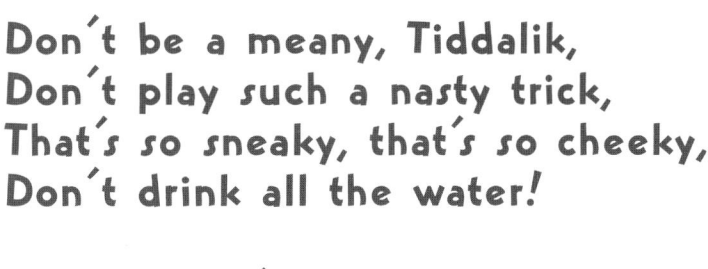

Don´t be a meany, Tiddalik,
Don´t play such a nasty trick,
That´s so sneaky, that´s so cheeky,
Don´t drink all the water!

No, no, don´t you think it!
No, no, don´t you drink it!
Water´s there for all to share,
So don´t drink all the water!

Forward to next track

But Tiddalik had a Great Big Thirst. Nothing was going to stop him.

SLURP, SLURP, SLURPITTY SLURP, GLUG, GLUG, GLUG!

His long tongue flickered in and out ... (ACTION.)

... and in moments, all that was left was mud.

The animals were really shocked. They shouted:

NOW LOOK WHAT YOU´VE GONE AND DONE! YOU´VE DRUNK IT ALL AND WE HAVE NONE!

But Tiddalik didn't care. And what's more, he was still thirsty. He looked around for something else to drink. (ACTION – TIDDALIK LOOKS AROUND.)

His eye fell on the deep, dark billabong. He said:

HMM. I´LL HAVE THAT!

The animals were horrified. They tried to hold him back. (ACTION.)

REPEAT CHORUS OF SONG: NO*! NO!*

No, no, don´t you think it ...

Forward to next track

But Tiddalik had a Great Big Thirst. He pushed them roughly out of the way.

SLURP, SLURP, SLURPITTY SLURP, GLUG, GLUG, GLUG!

And in no time at all, the billabong was empty. All that was left was mud. The animals were even more shocked!

NOW LOOK WHAT YOU'VE GONE AND DONE! YOU'VE DRUNK IT ALL AND WE HAVE NONE!

Did Tiddalik care? Not a bit. He looked around for something else to drink. (ACTION – TIDDALIK LOOKS AROUND.)

This time, his eye fell on the big blue lake. He said:

HMM. I'LL HAVE THAT!

The animals watched helplessly as he flopped towards the lake. (ACTION.) Yet again, they cried:

Forward to
next track

REPEAT CHORUS OF SONG: NO! NO!

No, no, don't you think it ...

But Tiddalik had a Great Big Thirst – and drink it he did.

SLURP, SLURP, SLURPITTY SLURP, GLUG, GLUG, GLUG!

And the water in the lake sank lower – and lower – and then it was gone. All that was left was mud.

NOW LOOK WHAT YOU'VE GONE AND DONE! YOU'VE DRUNK IT ALL AND WE HAVE NONE!

(ACTION – TIDDALIK FLOPS OVER TO HIS ROCK AND COLLAPSES.)

Scene 2: Bite him! Sting him!

The animals were really angry now. Possum said:

HE'S SOOOO SELFISH!

Emu said:

WE TOLD HIM TO STOP, BUT HE DIDN'T.

Script – TIDDALIK

Wombat said:

NOW THERE'S NOTHING TO DRINK.

Koala said:

HE'S DRUNK ALL THE WATER IN THE LAND.
I JUST HOPE HE'S SORRY.

And Tiddalik *was* sorry. For himself, that is. Because all that water was sloshing around down in his stomach. It was really heavy. He didn't feel at all well.

The four angry animals glared at him.

(ACTION – CROCODILE, SCORPION, KOOKABURRA AND KANGAROO WALK TOWARDS TIDDALIK.)

Tiddalik could see that they were furious. He would have liked to run away, but was so full of water he couldn't move!

Crocodile said:

I'LL BITE HIM!

Scorpion said:

I'LL STING HIM!

Kookaburra said:

I'LL PECK HIM!

Kangaroo said:

I'LL KICK HIM!

BITE HIM! STING HIM!
PECK HIM! KICK HIM!
MAKE HIM SCREAM AND SHOUT!

POKE HIM! PUSH HIM!
HIT HIM! HURT HIM!
GET THE WATER OUT!

Scene 3: Joke time

Tiddalik rolled his eyes in panic. Things were looking really bad.
But suddenly … Eel spoke up. He said:

I'VE GOT A BETTER IDEA. WHY DON'T WE TRY MAKING HIM LAUGH?

All the animals stopped. They looked at each other. Possum said:

I SUPPOSE WE COULD TRY. BUT HOW? (ACTION – SHRUG.)

The animals thought about how to make Tiddalik laugh. Wombat said:

I KNOW! I'LL TELL HIM A JOKE. WHO WAS THE FIRST UNDERWATER SPY?

The animals scratched their heads and said:

WHO?

Wombat said:

JAMES POND! (ACTION – EVERYONE LAUGHS.)

Everyone laughed and laughed. But Tiddalik didn't even smile. Emu said:

I'VE GOT ONE. WHERE DO FROGS KEEP THEIR SAVINGS?

The animals said:

WHERE?

Emu said:

IN THE RIVER BANK! (ACTION – EVERYONE LAUGHS.)

All the animals thought that was very funny. But Tiddalik still didn't smile.
Kangaroo said:

WHAT DO YOU CALL AN ANGRY FROG?

The animals said:

WHAT?

Script – TIDDALIK

Kangaroo said:

HOPPING MAD! (ACTION – EVERYONE LAUGHS.)

Everybody liked that one. Except Tiddalik. His mouth remained firmly closed. Eel said:

I DON'T THINK HE LIKES JOKES. WE MUST TRY SOMETHING ELSE.

Possum said:

LET'S TRY PULLING FUNNY FACES!

SONG: LET'S ALL PULL FUNNY FACES (*Original*)

Let's all pull funny faces,
Let's be silly and daft.
The last time we pulled funny faces,
Everyone laughed and laughed.

Let's all pull funny faces,
It makes you giggle and grin.
It's easily done, it's lots of fun ...
And everyone can join in.

Forward to
next track

So everyone pulled their funniest face. They wiggled their noses and poked out their tongues. (ACTION AND LAUGHTER.) Tiddalik just stared straight ahead. It seemed that nothing could make him laugh.

Scene 4: The Eel dance

Finally, Eel said:

NOTHING ELSE FOR IT. STAND BACK, EVERYONE. I SHALL NOW PERFORM THE FAMOUS EEL DANCE. WATCH MY MOVES, TIDDALIK.

And the dance began.

MUSIC: EEL DANCE (*Original*)

Forward to
next track

(ACTION – EEL PERFORMS A SILLY, WIGGLING DANCE. THE ANIMALS JOIN IN. EEL TWISTS HIMSELF INTO A TANGLE AND ENDS UP ON THE FLOOR.)

What a silly dance! Everyone joined in, wiggling and squiggling, twisting and turning. Eel was the best, though. He got so carried away that he overdid it, tied himself up in knots and ended up on the ground in a complete tangle!

There was a silence. (ACTION – THE ANIMALS FREEZE.)

Everyone looked at Tiddalik ...
(ACTION – THE ANIMALS ALL LOOK AT TIDDALIK, WHO SLOWLY HOPS OFF HIS ROCK AND MOVES TO THE FRONT.)

... and something happened. His mouth gave a twitch, and a few drops of water trickled out. (ACTION.)

Then he smiled, and the trickle became a stream. He gave a giggle, and the stream became a flood. And at long last – he laughed!

HA HA HA HA HA!

Water gushed from his mouth, filling the river ... the billabong ... and the lake!

REPEAT MUSIC: RAIN DANCE

Forward to next track

Finally, all the water that Tiddalik had guzzled was out of his tummy and back where it belonged. Tiddalik was really sorry about his Great Big Thirst. He said:

I'M REALLY SORRY.

He sounded like he meant it, too. So the animals forgave him. And from that time onwards, there was enough water for everybody. And now that Tiddalik had a whole lot of new friends – he couldn't stop laughing!

HA HA HA HA HA HA HA HA ...

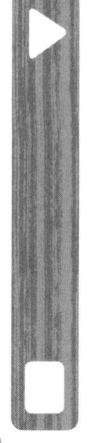

SONG: LAUGHTER WINS THE DAY (Original)

We hope you all enjoyed our play,
We hope it made you think.
Water's there for all to share
And everyone to drink.

We told some jokes and had some fun,
And sang along the way.
We hope you take the message home
That laughter wins the day.

Script – TIDDALIK

Performance Notes

☀ Staging and performance tips (see stage plan)

- Divide the cast into three groups, linked to the three water sources. Eel, Possum, Wombat, Emu, Koala and three dancers form the river group. They remain in the middle of the stage for most of the play. Crocodile, Kookaburra and three more dancers form the billabong group. They stand front right. Scorpion, Kangaroo and three dancers form the lake group. They stand front left. Divide any other animals between the billabong and the lake groups.

- **Scene 1:** the dancers, holding their water drapes, wait off-stage on the left, middle and right. Tiddalik is asleep on his rock. During the *Rain dance*, the dancers glide onto the stage, gently waving their drapes, and lay them on the floor – river down the middle, billabong front right and lake front left. They dance off and wait for their cue to remove the drapes.

- The animals move from their starting positions to their group's water source, where they pretend to drink. After *Thirsty*, Tiddalik clambers down from his rock. The animals return to their starting positions and sit down. Tiddalik waddles over to the river and pretends to drink. The river dancers slowly pull the drape off the stage. Tiddalik follows the drape, still pretending to drink. The same thing happens at the billabong and the lake. At the end of the scene, Tiddalik clambers back onto his rock.

- **Scene 2:** Crocodile, Kookaburra, Scorpion and Kangaroo move a little way towards Tiddalik, making threatening gestures.

- **Scene 3:** Eel suggests making Tiddalik laugh, and the four angry animals move back to their starting positions. Emu, Wombat and Koala stand up to tell their jokes.

- **Scene 4:** Wombat and Emu join Crocodile and Kookaburra on the right, and Koala and Possum join Kangaroo and Scorpion on the left, making room in the middle of the stage for Eel to perform his dance. The other animals wriggle and squirm around on the spot. The dancers bring back the water from the back of the stage. The river dancers pull their drape over the rock and Tiddalik's head, place it in its original position, and exit stage front. The billabong and lake dancers do the same, exiting stage right and left.

☀ Scenery

- Make a bush backcloth (see *Curriculum Links*).

Props

- Use a blue, silver or green sari for the water drapes. Make a raised rock for Tiddalik by covering a low PE table with a brown cloth.

Costumes

- Dress the children in plain, long-sleeved tops and trousers or tights, in colours appropriate to the animals they are representing. Make headbands (see *Curriculum Links*), and add the following distingushing features:

- **Tiddalik:** tuck trousers into long socks, and wear green or yellow rubber gloves on feet and hands. Stuff the front of Tiddalik's top with a small cushion after he has all drunk the water, and remove it at the end.

- **Eels:** white or black swimming hat or silver hood.

- **Possums and wombats:** grey or black mittens.

- **Crocodiles:** a strong, green refuse bag makes two tails. Cut diagonally, open the sealed end, stick or clip the unsealed length, and stuff. Decorate with paper or painted scales. Wear rubber gloves with stuffed fingers on feet and hands.

- **Scorpions:** to create the effect of segments and pincers, put a pair of inflated swimming arm bands on each arm – one above the elbow, the other below. Wear a large, long-sleeved T-shirt over the top and tie shoelaces round each elbow and wrist. Make a pointed tail by stuffing one leg of a pair of tights and painting a red sting on the end. Secure at the back with safety pins.

- **Kookaburras:** make white bibs for the kookaburras' chests. For the wings, cut out a large, brown fabric triangle and stick, sew or staple brown and grey feathers to one side. Gather two corners of each triangle with elastic bands – these are held in the children's hands. Attach the middle fold of the wings to the back of the tops.

- **Kangaroos:** wear tops with large pockets to represent pouches, and brown mittens.

- **Emus:** wear orange rubber gloves with stuffed fingers on feet. Make grey tail feathers out of tissue or crepe paper, and attach them to the back of a tape waistband so that the feathers hang over the back of the emus' legs.

- **Koalas:** make fluffy brown bibs for the koalas' chests.

- **Rain dancers:** attach strips of white or blue plastic to lengths of wide tape to make rain skirts.

Sound effects

- **Tiddalik's drinking chant:** half fill plastic bottles with water and slosh them around.

Teaching Notes – TIDDALIK

Curriculum Links

PSHE

- Tiddalik's selfishness made the animals angry. What did they threaten to do? Things were looking pretty bad when Eel said, 'I've got a better idea. Why don't we try making him laugh?' Did Eel's idea work?

- Ask the children to think of some situations that could lead others to act selfishly in school. Act them out in groups, one at a time. Invite observers to comment on what can be done to resolve the problem. For example, a group of children are drawing daffodils. One child has taken all the yellow pastels and won't let anyone else have them. Reactions from the other children in the group might include telling the teacher, forcing the child's fingers open to release the pastels, getting more yellow pastels from another table, asking the child why she or he won't share the pastels, or offering to swap the yellows for another colour. Try the suggestions out one at a time, and ask the child playing the part of the selfish pupil how they make him or her feel. Was there a best solution?

Literacy

- Ask the children about their favourite funny stories or poems. Invite them to find extracts that really make them laugh and read them to the rest of the class. Why do they find these bits so funny?

- Invite children to tell their favourite jokes. Talk about the importance of speaking clearly and delivering punch lines with a flourish.

- Read the children some more Aboriginal stories and legends.

Science

- Water is essential for plant growth. People need fruits, seeds and vegetables to live. Some countries don't have a lot of rain and this can lead to famine. In our country we usually have enough rain, but sometimes, in hot weather, we have to try to save water.

- How can we save water? (Eg, have a shower rather than a bath, don't leave the tap running when cleaning teeth or washing dishes, don't use paddling pools.)

☼ Geography

- Find Australia on a globe or map. How far away from the UK is it? How long does it take to fly to Australia from the UK? What countries might you fly over?

- Make a list of the Australian bush animals mentioned in the story of *Tiddalik*. Use reference books and the internet to find out more about them. What do they look like? What do they eat? Where do they live? Do they only live in Australia? Draw or paint them.

☼ History

- Talk about the transportation of prisoners to Australia in the 19th century and the Aborigines who lived in Australia for thousands of years before people from other countries started to colonise it. Look at examples of Aboriginal art. Encourage the children to research these topics at home.

☼ Art and Design

- Make animal headbands for the play. Research the animals and make drawings of their heads from the front. Ask the children to pick out one distinctive feature of each animal to make into a headband, eg, Kookaburra's beak, Crocodile's eyes and mouth, or Koala's ears. Think about the colours needed, and what could be added to make the headbands exciting, eg, fur fabric, wool, string, black plastic and buttons. Sketch the animal features on strong, A4 card. Paint and decorate, cut out, and staple to strong strips of card. Alternatively, make sketches of the animals' whole heads, decorate, cut out, and attach to headbands.

- Make a backdrop for the play, which is set in the Australian bush after a drought. Measure and cut out paper or fabric to fit a display board. (The fabric used for roller blinds makes a good backcloth.) Sponge print a blue sky. Use decorating rollers and brown and yellow paint to create an arid background. Print scrubby bushes and skeletal trees using sides of rulers dipped in brown and black paint. Use small pieces of stiff card to print the twigs and thorns. Cut large and medium-sized boulders out of brown parcel paper or sugar paper. Partially staple them to the display board, and then stuff with tissue paper to bulk them out.

Monster Ps and Qs by Veronica Clark

Cast

Storytellers (1 adult or 4 children)
Mr and Mrs Monster
Grimlock
The twins, Jangle and Yomper
Gnaw, the Monsters' dog
Pedestrians (at least 3)

People in bus queue (at least 3)
Bus driver
Friendly neighbour
Football referee
Footballers (11)

All the named characters, the people in the bus queue, and the neighbour have speaking parts. Use a doll for Dribbola, the Monsters' baby. If an adult takes the role of storyteller, increase the number of pedestrians and bus passengers.

Assembly theme

The theme of *Monster Ps and Qs* is courtesy. The final song sums up the message that good manners encourage a polite response.

Story

The Monster family (apart from Grimlock) think that rudeness should be encouraged, so Grimlock is horrified when he learns that his family intends to come to watch his football match. On the way to the bus stop, his parents barge into people and attempt to push to the front of the bus queue, but the wind is taken out of Mr Monster's sails when a passer by praises his children.

At the football ground, Mr Monster is ashamed when Grimlock runs to help a player on the opposite team who trips over. He doesn't know how to react when the referee compliments him on the good manners of his son. However, Mrs Monster blushes with pleasure to hear her eldest child praised.

Back at home, Mr Monster is clearly outnumbered when not only his children, but also his wife, start speaking and acting politely. Finally, Mr Monster is heard to mutter a reluctant, 'Yes, please.'

Setting

The play begins and ends in the Monsters' living room. After breakfast, the Monster family makes its way to the football ground.

Songs and dances

We don't say thank you is sung four times. The first verse is always sung by one or more of the Monsters, and everybody joins in with the second verse. At the end of the play, the Monsters dance through the audience to the *Monster Stomp*.

Script: Monster Ps and Qs

Scene 1: Breakfast

Forward to next track

MUSIC: MONSTER STOMP (Original)

(ACTION – DURING THE MONSTER STOMP, THE MONSTER CHILDREN TUCK INTO THEIR BREAKFASTS. MR MONSTER READS THE PAPER AND MRS MONSTER CUDDLES THE BABY.)

STORYTELLER 1
Grimlock carefully spread the butter right to the corners of his piece of toast. (ACTION.)

GRIMLOCK
Mum, pass the wormalade, please.

STORYTELLER 1
Mrs Monster shrieked and dropped the spoon of porridge she was putting into Baby Monster's mouth. (ACTION.)

MRS MONSTER
What did you say?

STORYTELLER 1
Grimlock looked up and sighed.

GRIMLOCK
(SIGHS.)
Pass the wormalade, please.

(ACTION –THE TWINS OPEN THEIR MOUTHS WIDE IN HORROR. GNAW CRAWLS BEHIND MR MONSTER'S CHAIR AND PUTS HIS PAWS OVER HIS EARS.)

STORYTELLER 1
Mr Monster threw down his paper, hauled Grimlock out of his chair by the scruff of his hairy neck, and growled:

MR MONSTER
Go to your room at once. I will not have the p-word spoken in this house!

(ACTION – THE MONSTER TWINS SNIGGER BEHIND THEIR HANDS.)

GRIMLOCK
B ... b ... b ... but, teacher says we should be polite!

MR MONSTER
Never mind what teacher says. Monsters are rude, and that's that!

(ACTION – GRIMLOCK HANGS HIS HEAD AND GOES TO SIT BEHIND MR MONSTER'S CHAIR.)

CD 43/52

SONG: WE DON'T SAY THANK YOU (*Adapted from The hokey cokey*)

▶

∥ Forward to
next track

(THE MONSTERS)
We don't say THANK YOU and we don't say PLEASE,
We don't say AFTER YOU.
We never, ever say I'M SORRY,
HELLO and HOW D'YOU DO?

(EVERYONE)
They don't say THANK YOU and they don't say PLEASE,
They don't say AFTER YOU.
They never, ever say I'M SORRY,
HELLO and HOW D'YOU DO?

Scene 2: The bus queue

STORYTELLER 2
Later that day, the Monster family set off for the town. Grimlock had been chosen to play on his school six-a-side football team. To his horror, his mum and dad said they would come along and watch.

Mr and Mrs Monster and the twins stormed down the street. Mrs Monster used the pushchair like a tank, sending people and shopping bags flying. (ACTION.)

Grimlock walked behind, gathering up shopping and whispering, 'Sorry, sorry'. (ACTION.)

Mr Monster looked back to see what Grimlock was up to.

MR MONSTER
Grimlock! What do you think you're doing? Get back here!

(ACTION – STILL APOLOGISING UNDER HIS BREATH, GRIMLOCK CATCHES UP WITH THE MONSTERS.)

STORYTELLER 2

As they approached the bus stop, Grimlock's heart sank. There was a queue – and monsters are not good at queuing.

The bus arrived. Mr Monster was just about to shove the little old lady in front of him out of the way, when she turned round and said:

OLD LADY

Oh what darling children. And so many of them! You must go straight to the front of the queue.

STORYTELLER 2

Firmly holding the hands of the Monster twins, the lady marched them past all the other people. To the amazement of Mr and Mrs Monster, everyone smiled and made way for them.

PEOPLE IN BUS QUEUE

After you. Please go first.

STORYTELLER 2

Grimlock whispered 'thank you'. Jangle chirped up with a 'thank you' too.

Mr Monster was furious. When they were sitting down, he bent down and hissed in the children's ears:

 **REPEAT SONG: WE DON'T SAY THANK YOU**

(MR AND MRS MONSTER)
We don't say THANK YOU ...

Forward to next track

Scene 3: The football match

STORYTELLER 3

When they reached the football ground, Grimlock went to join his team and the Monster family joined the other spectators on the sidelines. Mr Monster ripped open a bar of chocolate and threw the shiny paper onto the grass. (ACTION.)

A man standing near him picked it up and handed it to Mr Monster, saying:

SPECTATOR 1

This wind is quite a nuisance, isn't it?

SPECTATOR 2

Hope it doesn't spoil the match.

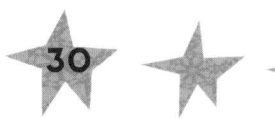

Script – MONSTER PS AND QS

STORYTELLER 3
Mr Monster scowled and shoved the paper into his pocket. (ACTION.)

(ACTION – THE TWO CAPTAINS AND THE REFEREE ENTER THE STAGE AREA. THE REFEREE STANDS NEAR MR AND MRS MONSTER.)

As he ran out onto the field, the captain of the other team tripped over his laces. Grimlock stopped and helped him to his feet. (ACTION.)

MRS MONSTER
That boy is a disgrace to the family.

STORYTELLER 3
The referee turned to her and said:

REFEREE
Nice lad you have there. You must be proud of him.

STORYTELLER 3
Mrs Monster went pink and almost managed a smile. The referee blew his whistle, and the match started.

(ACTION – THE REST OF THE PLAYERS JOG ONTO THE PITCH AND RUN AROUND, KICKING A BALL. THE SPECTATORS CHEER THEM ON. A WHISTLE SIGNALS THE END OF THE MATCH. THE PLAYERS SHAKE HANDS AND JOG BACK TO THEIR BENCHES. THE SPECTATORS RETURN TO THEIR STARTING POSITIONS. GRIMLOCK JOINS HIS FAMILY.)

Scene 4: Back home

STORYTELLER 4
At the end of the match, the Monsters made their way home.

(ACTION – THE MONSTERS WALK HOME THE SAME WAY THEY CAME. THEY MEET THEIR NEIGHBOUR IN THE MIDDLE OF THE STAGE.)

They were just turning into their street when they met the man who lived at number 45. He smiled and said:

NEIGHBOUR
How do you do?

GRIMLOCK
How d'you do?

NEIGHBOUR
Had a good match?

GRIMLOCK
Yes thank you.

JANGLE
We won 3–nil.

YOMPER
And Grimlock scored a goal!

(ACTION – NEIGHBOUR SMILES AND CONTINUES ON HIS WAY ACROSS
THE STAGE.)

STORYTELLER 4
By this time, Mr Monster was hopping up and down with fury.
As they walked up to their front door, he snarled:

REPEAT SONG: WE DON'T SAY THANK YOU

(MR MONSTER)
We don't say THANK YOU ...

Forward to
next track

STORYTELLER 4
When the twins reached the open door, they stood to one side and said:

MONSTER TWINS
After you, mum.

MRS MONSTER
Thank you ...

STORYTELLER 4
Inside, Mr Monster slumped in his chair, closed his eyes, and sulked. (ACTION.)

Mrs Monster started to prepare the stew. She hummed as she peeled the
potatoes. (ACTION.)

Grimlock entertained the baby. Yomper and Jangle set the table.
Gnaw fetched Mr Monster's slippers and laid them at his feet. (ACTION.)

When Mr Monster opened his eyes he was surprised to see his slippers by his
feet. He opened his mouth to say, 'Thank y…', and stopped just in time. (ACTION.)

Putting his hand to his head, he groaned. What was happening to his
rude Monster family? The children even *looked* different.

(ACTION – THE REST OF THE FAMILY SMILE AT EACH OTHER.)

Script – MONSTER PS AND QS

During supper, there were quite a few 'pleases' and 'thank yous', and even a 'sorry' when Grimlock dropped some stew. The words just slipped out. But it was when Baby Monster said 'More stoo peas,' that Mr Monster finally lost it. He threw down his spoon and shouted –

REPEAT SONG: WE DON'T SAY THANK YOU

(MR MONSTER)
We don't say THANK YOU ...

REST OF THE MONSTER FAMILY
BUT WE DO!

SONG: WE DO SAY THANK YOU (*Original*)

We do say THANK YOU and we do say PLEASE ...
We always say I'M SORRY ...

STORYTELLER 4
Mr Monster groaned, and flopped down into his chair. (ACTION.)

GRIMLOCK
Would you like the paper? (ACTION – GRIMLOCK HOLDS OUT THE PAPER.)

MR MONSTER
(GRUDGINGLY BUT CLEARLY.) Yes please.

(ACTION – EVERYONE STANDS UP AND CHEERS.)

SONG: COURTESY IS CATCHING (*Original*)

Courtesy is catching,
Like measles, mumps and flu.
If you're polite to others,
They're polite to you.
Smile at people, say hello,
Mind your Ps and Qs.
Open doors, show you care.
Polite or rude ... you choose.

REPEAT MUSIC: MONSTER STOMP

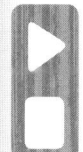

(ACTION – THE MONSTERS AND GNAW LEAVE THE STAGE. THEY PAUSE TO SHAKE HANDS WITH MEMBERS OF THE AUDIENCE, CALLING OUT PLEASANTRIES, SUCH AS 'THANKS FOR COMING!')

Performance Notes

Staging and performance tips (see stage plan)

- The play starts and finishes in the Monsters' living room (which, if possible, is on a raised stage). In Scenes 2 and 3, the floor-level stage area in front of the living room is the route to the football pitch, and in Scene 3 it becomes the football pitch and sideline. Stick tape across the stage to represent the sideline: this will help the spectators to find their places.

- *Scene 1*: when the Monsters leave the house for the football match, Mrs Monster and the baby lead the way, with Grimlock bringing up the rear.

- *Scene 2*: as the Monsters leave their house, the pedestrians walk slowly across the middle of the stage towards the Monsters' front door. Mrs Monster barges through them. The pedestrians limp to the steps of the house and sit down until the start of the match.

- The bus arrives from the left, and the people in the bus queue stand up, facing the front. The Monsters face the bus driver and crouch as though sitting, and the polite passengers take up their positions behind them, facing the audience.

- *Scene 3*: Grimlock leaves the bus and joins his team. The pedestrians stand up and join the Monsters and the other bus passengers on the sideline of the football pitch. The friendly neighbour moves to the far end of the bench on the right, where he waits for his cue. The Monsters push their way to the middle of the stage. The bus drives off stage right and the bus stop sign is removed.

- *Scene 4*: at the beginning of this scene, the friendly neighbour enters on the right and walks over to the middle of the stage. After exchanging pleasantries with Grimlock, he exits stage left.

- The narrator describing the Monsters getting ready for dinner should leave plenty of time for them to perform their actions. Mr Monster is the only one to sing (or growl) the first verse of *We don't say thank you*. The rest of the cast, however, sing the second verse with great enthusiasm. Everyone stands to sing *Courtesy is catching*.

Props

- Make the bottom part of the side of a bus out of strong card, about two metres long and waist height. Print the slogan 'Courtesy is catching' above the wheels. The bus driver and one of the people in the queue hold the bus upright.

In the Monsters' kitchen:
- Doll (Baby Monster – Dribbola).
- Toy high chair.
- Small table and three small chairs.
- Chair with cushions for Mr Monster.
- Five plastic bowls and spoons.
- Box of Cheat-a-bix.
- Toast, butter and jar of wormalade.
- Newspaper.
- Potatoes, peeler and pan.
- Slippers for Mr Monster.

In town:
- Toy pushchair for Dribbola.
- Shopping bags for pedestrians.
- Bus stop sign – make the sign out of strong card and mount on a rounders post.
- Bar of chocolate with shiny wrapper.

Costumes

- **The Monsters:** casual, scruffy clothing, except Grimlock, who wears an immaculate football kit. All the Monsters, including the baby, wear brightly coloured, curly wigs.

- **Football players and referee:** football kits.

- **Bus driver:** dark jacket, long trousers and peaked cap.

- **Everyone else:** casual clothing with optional football scarves for spectators.

Sound effects

- Find a whistle for the football match.

- Use gravel in a plastic pot to make a bus engine sound. As the bus approaches, increase the volume, and as it drives off, get quieter.

# Curriculum Links

Literacy Link
Stories about fantasy worlds.

PSHE

- Ask the children to practise saying some of the rude things the Monsters said in *Monster Ps and Qs.* (For example, 'Never mind what teacher says!' or, 'We don't say thank you.') Can they match facial expression, body language and tone of voice to the words? Do the same with some of the polite phrases in the play. (For example, 'Pass the wormalade, please,' or, 'Nice lad you have there.')

> ### ACTIVITY BOX: HOW POLITE!
> Write down some tricky situations on pieces of card, eg:
> - Someone pushes me over in the playground.
> - My friend comes to tea. There's only one biscuit left on the plate and we'd both like to eat it.
> - I reach a door at the same time as my friend and there's only room for one of us to go through.
> - My friend comes to school in a new coat and I don't like it very much.
>
> Fold the cards in two. Put them in an open box and invite a child to pick one and read out loud what's written on it. The child then tries to think of a polite thing to say in response to the situation. Act out the scene, including the polite response. Repeat with another card.

Courtesy week

- Have a courtesy week. Each time a member of staff or a child reports someone being polite, put a marble in a jar. When the jar is full, give the children a reward, such as an extra playtime.

PE

- In a large space, practise impolite body language. Half the children in the class find a space and stand still. Without touching, speaking or making any noise, the remaining children move round the room behaving impolitely to the standing children; they pretend to shove them, turn their backs on them and pull faces.

- Now repeat the activity, but this time use polite body language. Shake hands, walk round the static children without pushing, look them in the eyes and smile. This time, allow speaking. Gather together to discuss the experience.

The Mirror of Truth by Veronica Clark

Cast

Storyteller (adult)	Head Gardener
King Belvedere	Chief Guard
Oliver, Grenville and Georgie	Palace servants (about 7)
(the King's personal assistants)	Gardeners (about 7)
Head Cook	Guards (about 8)

Assembly theme

The Mirror of Truth describes the benefits of a healthy lifestyle. The emphasis is on exercise, although there are references to diet and eating habits.

Story

King Belevdere has let himself go: poor diet and lack of exercise means he has piled on the pounds. Glancing in the mirror, he refuses to believe that the chubby man in the reflection is really himself. He orders the mirror to be thrown out.

His canny assistants, Oliver, Georgie and Grenville, devise a plan to get the king back into good shape. They tell King Belvedere that if he wants to see what he really looks like, he must find the magic Mirror of Truth. The king orders his staff to search the palace, but no mirror is found. His assistants inform him that the Mirror of Truth only reveals a true image to the person who finds it – in other words, the king must look for it himself. Reluctantly, Belvedere searches the palace grounds, but can't find the mirror. Over the next few weeks, King Belvedere makes longer and longer treks into the surrounding countryside in search of the magic mirror.

When the inspection of the guards comes round again, the ceremonial jacket fits perfectly. The king's assistants decide that it's time to tell the king about their plan. They fetch the old mirror from the back of the wardrobe and place it in front of the king. He is delighted when he sees a fit and healthy man. He thinks that he has finally found the Mirror of Truth, until his assistants tell him that it is actually his old mirror.

Setting

The play starts and finishes in the king's private rooms. In between, the audience is taken through the palace, out into the grounds, and further afield – all in the search for the Mirror of Truth.

Songs

There are three songs, two of which are sung to familiar tunes. *Where's the mirror?* can be split between everyone and the king, as indicated in the script, or it can be sung straight through by everyone.

Script: The Mirror of Truth

Scene 1: Get rid of it!

STORYTELLER
King Belvedere popped a chocolate into his mouth, pulled his crown over his eyes, and settled down for a snooze in his favourite armchair.

(ACTION – WHILE THE KING SNOOZES, HIS GUARDS, SERVANTS AND GARDENERS ARE HARD AT WORK.)

(SOUND EFFECT – CLOCK CHIMES MIDDAY.)

On the stroke of midday, his three personal assistants, Oliver, Georgie and Grenville, entered the king's room. Oliver shook him gently. (ACTION.)

OLIVER
Wake up, Your Majesty. It's time for the inspection of the guard.

KING BELVEDERE
(YAWNING.)
Uugh – do I have to get up?

ASSISTANTS
Yes, Your Majesty.

STORYTELLER
Oliver pulled the king out of his chair. (ACTION.)

Georgie helped him into ceremonial jacket. It was quite a struggle. (ACTION.)

Grenville straightened his crown. (ACTION.)

As he shuffled out of the room in his slippers, King Belvedere passed the mirror. He glanced into it, and gave a cry of amazement. (ACTION.)

KING BELVEDERE
Is that *me*?!

ASSISTANTS
(NERVOUSLY.)
Yes, Your Majesty.

 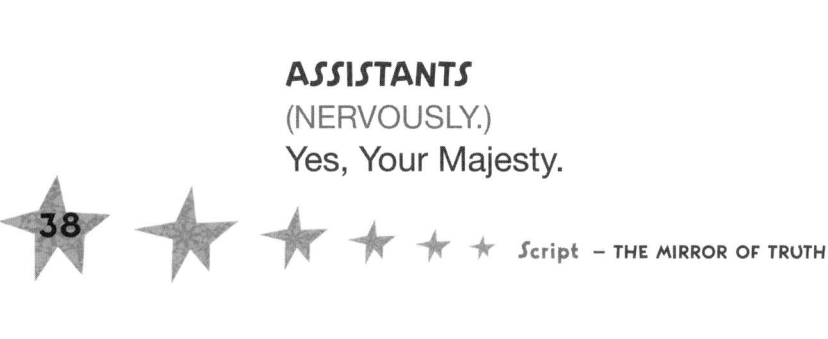

KING BELVEDERE
Rubbish! I'm young and handsome. What a stupid mirror. Get rid of it.

(ACTION – THE THREE ASSISTANTS WAIT UNTIL THE KING HAS SHUFFLED OUT OF THE ROOM, THEN HIDE THE MIRROR.)

Scene 2: Do I look fit?

STORYTELLER
On the way to the drill yard, the king passed through the palace. Walking over to the Head Cook, King Belvedere said, in his most commanding voice:

KING BELVEDERE
Head Cook, do I look fit?

(ACTION – HEAD COOK BOWS.)

HEAD COOK
Yes, Your Majesty.

STORYTELLER
Passing through the palace gardens, the king asked the Head Gardener the same question.

KING BELVEDERE
Head Gardener, do I look fit?

(ACTION – HEAD GARDENER BOWS.)

HEAD GARDENER
Yes, Your Majesty.

STORYTELLER
The king gave the palace guards a quick inspection and returned to his chamber.

(ACTION – THE KING RETURNS TO HIS CHAMBER, HAVING GIVEN ONLY A CURSORY GLANCE AT THE GUARDS.)

STORYTELLER
Later that day, as he slumped in his chair munching biscuits, King Belvedere couldn't stop thinking about the mirror that made him look so awful. He turned to Oliver, who was sewing buttons on his jacket, and said, 'Oliver, did you get rid of that stupid mirror?'

Oliver looked up and said, 'Yes, Your Majesty.'

He paused, then added, 'But maybe you should replace it with the Mirror of Truth. The Mirror of Truth never lies.'

The King looked thoughtful, then ordered Oliver to fetch the mirror. Oliver shook his head and said, 'I can't do that, Your Majesty. First you have to find it!'

Scene 3: Searching for the mirror

STORYTELLER
King Belvedere ordered everyone in the palace to search for the Mirror of Truth.

The guards searched their barracks.

(ACTION – DURING THE SONG, THE GUARDS MILL AROUND THEIR SECTION OF THE STAGE, SEARCHING HIGH AND LOW, THEN RETURN TO THEIR PLACES.)

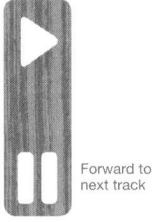
Forward to next track

SONG: SEARCHING (*In and out the dusky bluebells*)

In and out the boots and helmets,
In and out the boots and helmets,
In and out the boots and helmets,
Searching for a mirror.

STORYTELLER
The Chief Guard reported to the king.

CHIEF GUARD
(ACTION – BOWS.)
No mirror, Your Majesty.

STORYTELLER
The servants searched every room in the palace.

(ACTION – DURING THE SONG, THE PALACE SERVANTS SEARCH THE BACK OF THE STAGE, THEN RETURN TO THEIR LINES.)

REPEAT SONG: SEARCHING

Forward to next track

In and out the halls and kitchens,
In and out the halls and kitchens,
In and out the halls and kitchens,
Searching for a mirror.

STORYTELLER
The Head Cook reported to the king.

HEAD COOK
(ACTION – BOWS.)
No mirror, Your Majesty.

STORYTELLER
The gardeners searched the palace grounds.

(ACTION – DURING THE SONG, THE GARDENERS SEARCH IN FRONT OF THE STAGE, THEN RETURN TO THEIR LINES.)

REPEAT SONG: SEARCHING

Forward to next track

In and out the trees and fountains,
In and out the trees and fountains,
In and out the trees and fountains,
Searching for a mirror.

STORYTELLER
The Head Gardener reported to the king.

HEAD GARDENER
(ACTION – BOWS.)
No mirror, Your Majesty.

Scene 4: Where, oh where?

STORYTELLER
The next day, King Belvedere was rooting around in a box of chocolates, looking for the soft centres, when Georgie tapped him on the shoulder.

Georgie bowed, and said, 'Your Majesty, there is something we must tell you about the Mirror of Truth.'

The King looked up. Georgie continued, 'The Mirror of Truth is a magic mirror. It will only show a true image to the person who finds it.'

The King choked on his strawberry cream. 'What?' he cried. 'You mean *I* have to go around looking for a mirror?'

ASSISTANTS
Yes, Your Majesty.

STORYTELLER
The king put on a sulky face.

At eleven o'clock the next morning, King Belvedere and his assistants went to search the palace again. (ACTION.)

They looked everywhere.

(ACTION – DURING THE SONG, THE KING AND HIS ASSISTANTS SPLIT UP TO SEARCH THE PALACE, THE GROUNDS AND THE GUARDS' BARRACKS.)

SONG: WHERE'S THE MIRROR? *(Stand off)*

(ALL)
Searching here and searching there,
(KING)
Where's the mirror? Where oh where?
(ALL)
Up and down and round about,
(KING)
If you find it, give a shout.

STORYTELLER
But no mirror was to be found.

(ACTION – THE KING FLOPS DOWN IN HIS ARMCHAIR AND FALLS ASLEEP.)

STORYTELLER

That night the king slept well, and in the morning he ate a good breakfast of porridge and toast. (ACTION.)

At ten o'clock, he swapped his slippers for a pair of shoes, and, accompanied by his guards, set out to search the woods around the palace.

(ACTION – DURING THE SONG, THE KING AND THE GUARDS MARCH AWAY FROM THE STAGE AND SEARCH FOR THE MIRROR.)

CD 65/73

Forward to
next track

REPEAT SONG: WHERE'S THE MIRROR?

Searching here and searching there ...

(ACTION – DURING THE FOLLOWING NARRATIVE, THE KING CHANGES INTO A PAIR OF RUNNING SHOES AND JOGS UP AND DOWN ON THE SPOT.)

STORYTELLER

By now the palace was humming with the news of the king's search for the Mirror of Truth. When the king, wearing a smart pair of running shoes and shorts, left the palace at seven o'clock to search the nearby hills, he was followed by the guards, the cooks, the scullery maids, the butlers and the chamber maids.

(ACTION – DURING THE SONG, THE KING AND HIS STAFF JOG AROUND THE HALL WITH ENTHUSIASM.)

CD 66/74

Forward to
next track

REPEAT SONG: WHERE'S THE MIRROR?

Searching here and searching there ...

STORYTELLER

This went on for some time. The king began to look forward to his daily exercise, and developed quite a love of the countryside.

(ACTION – THE KING AND HIS ENTOURAGE RETURN TO THEIR STARTING POSITIONS.)

Each evening, he would sink into his chair by the fire with a mug of hot chocolate and do the palace crossword. (ACTION.)

Scene 5: Fit and healthy

STORYTELLER
Four weeks went by, and it was once again time for the monthly inspection of the guards.

(SOUND EFFECT – CLOCK CHIMES MIDDAY.)

The king's assistants helped him into his ceremonial clothes – and this time, the jacket slipped on quite easily. (ACTION.)

King Belvedere completed his tour in just one hour.

(ACTION – KING BELVEDERE TAKES THE SAME ROUTE AS BEFORE, BUT THIS TIME HE WALKS BRISKLY AND GREETS HIS SERVANTS CHEERFULLY.)

Later in the day, as King Belvedere was sitting in front of the fire doing the crossword in the *Palace Weekly*, he had a visit from his assistants.

(ACTION – GRENVILLE COUGHS DISCRETELY TO ATTRACT THE KING'S ATTENTION.)

GRENVILLE
Your Majesty, we have something to tell you.

STORYTELLER
The king mumbled to himself, '10 across. Who looks really fit and is much better tempered? Two words, 4 and 9.'

ASSISTANTS
Your Majesty, there is no Mirror of Truth.

KING BELVEDERE
(SUDDENLY PAYING ATTENTION.)
I beg your pardon?

ASSISTANTS
THERE IS NO MIRROR OF TRUTH!

(ACTION – THE KING STARES AT HIS ASSISTANTS IN SURPRISE.)

We made it up.

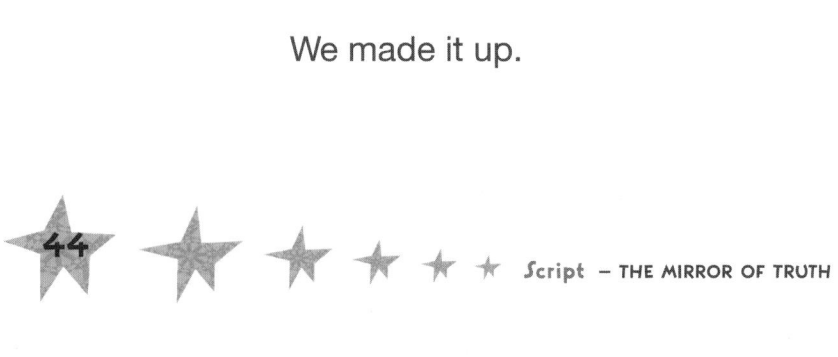

STORYTELLER
Grenville walked over to the wardrobe and brought out the mirror they had hidden. (ACTION.)

He dragged it over to the king. King Belvedere stood up and looked at his reflection. (ACTION.)

He saw a strong, rosy-cheeked young man.

KING BELVEDERE
But this *is* the Mirror of Truth! It was in my wardrobe all the time.

GRENVILLE
No, Your Majesty, it's your old mirror. But a month ago, you didn't want to believe what you saw.

STORYTELLER
King Belvedere sat back in his chair and roared with laughter. (ACTION.)

(ACTION – EVERYONE JOINS IN WITH THE FINAL SONG. JOG IN TIME TO THE MUSIC IN LINES 1 AND 3 OF EACH VERSE.)

CD 67/75

SONG: FIT AND HEALTHY (*Original*)

What do you get if you exercise?
Rosy cheeks and shining eyes,
That's what you get if you exercise,
Hip, hip, hip, hooray.

What do you get if you exercise?
A healthy heart and sturdy thighs,
That's what you get if you exercise,
Hip, hip, hip, hooray.

What do you get if you exercise?
A good night's sleep and an appetite,
That's what you get if you exercise,
Hip, hip, hip, hooray.

Performance Notes

☼ Staging and performance tips (see stage plan)

- King Belvedere and his three assistants are on a small raised stage to the right of the main stage area. The palace guards stand to attention in two lines below the king's chamber. The head cook and palace servants stand along the back of the main stage area, with the head gardener and his staff along the front. The gardeners kneel or squat down so that the palace servants can be seen.

- Scene 1: at the start of the play, we see the servants and guards at work: scrubbing, scraping, polishing, digging and weeding. King Belvedere, attended by his three faithful assistants, is snoozing in his chair. Everyone stops what they are doing and keeps still while the king and his assistants are speaking.

- At the end of the scene, the king tells his assistants to get rid of the mirror. They can either cover it with a drape, place it on the floor behind the raised platform, or both.

- Scene 2: the route to the barracks takes the king down the steps from his chambers and across the back of the stage from right to left, where he passes the palace servants. Then he turns and walks back across the stage in front of the gardeners. He makes a cursory inspection of the guards before returning to his armchair.

- As the king approaches, the palace servants stand up straight and bob, bow or salute. The gardeners stand up after the king has addressed the Head Cook and crouch or kneel again when the king moves over to the guards. When the king is back in his chamber, Oliver sits on a stool, sewing. Georgie and Grenville stand on the right.

- Scene 3: on the orders of the king, the guards, palace servants and gardeners take it in turn to search for the Mirror of Truth. They bustle around in their area of the stage during the verses of *Searching* that refer to them. The Chief Guard, Head Cook and Head Gardener stand on the steps between the stages to report to the king.

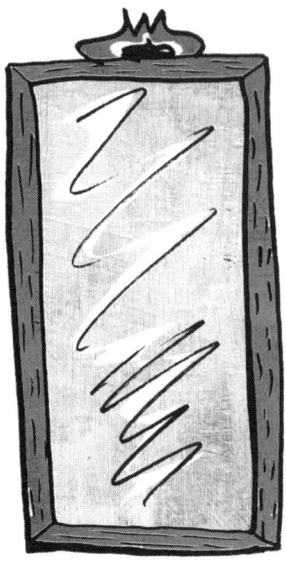

- Scene 4: While the king is rooting through his chocolates, the three assistants get into a huddle to discuss their next course of action. Georgie breaks away to talk to the king.

- In the final search, the king and his entire staff jog around the back and sides of the hall and up and down the central aisle. At the end of the song, the actors return to their starting places.

- **Scene 5:** as they get the king ready for the palace inspection, the three assistants repeat the dressing procedure described in Scene 1. Taking the same inspection route as before, King Belvedere briskly walks to the drill yard, calling out cheery greetings to his heads of staff.

- While the king is doing his crossword, the assistants once again get into a huddle. This time it is Grenville's turn to confront the king with some startling information.

Scenery

- Place a couple of tall potted plants at each side of the front of the stage, to represent the palace gardens.

Props

- An armchair draped with velvet or gold cloth, small stool, ceremonial jacket and crown, freestanding mirror.
- Box of chocolates, packet of biscuits, mug of chocolate.
- Newspaper.
- **Servants:** feather dusters and small bowls and spoons.
- **Gardeners:** trowels and baskets.

Costumes

- **King Belvedere:** wears a fancy belt, slippers, ceremonial jacket and crown. In Scene 4, he changes his footwear twice; first he abandons his slippers for shoes, then changes into trainers.

- **Palace servants, gardeners and three assistants:** white shirts, black trousers or skirts, and black shoes, plimsolls or boots. Give the female servants white aprons and lacy caps. The Head Cook can wear a tall chef's hat. The gardeners wear neck scarves and green aprons. The assistants could also wear coloured sashes round their waists and tuck their trousers into long, brightly striped socks.

- **The Guards:** red or black long or short sleeved tops, with red tights or black trousers and plimsolls. Make tunics out of strong, black plastic bags. Cut holes for head and arms, adjust the length, and tie round the waist with belts or tape. Make helmet headbands (cover the helmet shape with silver foil).

Curriculum Links

Literacy Link
Traditional and fairy tales.

PSHE/Science

Exercise

- King Belvedere was overweight, pasty, tired and bad-tempered. He also snacked a lot. After regular exercise, he became trimmer, improved his eating habits, had a good colour and was better tempered.

- Ask the children which muscles King Belvedere exercised when he went running.

The heart

- Tell the children about their hearts – muscles inside their bodies that can't be seen but which need regular exercise. The heart helps every other part of the body work efficiently. It pumps blood all the way round the body. Look at a chart showing the inside of a body. Locate the heart and track the journey of blood round the body through arteries, veins and capillaries.

- Talk about what happens to the heart when we exercise. During exercise, the heart has to work hard in order to pump extra blood to the muscles being used. All types of activity – walking briskly, running, jumping, dancing and swimming – exercise the heart. Children should take part in some form of vigorous exercise every day.

ACTIVITY BOX: BEFORE AND AFTER

Ask the children to get into pairs. Ask them to look closely at their partners' faces and note their colour. Next, ask them to feel their partners' foreheads – are they warm or cool, dry or damp? Show them how to listen to heart beats by putting one ear against their partners' chests. Note the speed of their partners' breathing.

Now move to an area where the children can run without stopping for two or three minutes. Alternatively, they can skip with a rope for one minute.

Back inside the classroom, ask the children to repeat the things they did before exercising: note changes in face colour, the temperature and feel of foreheads, and the rate of heartbeats and breathing.

☀ Art and Design

- Provide the children with hand-held mirrors, pencil crayons or pastels and white A4 sugar paper. Ask them to look carefully at their reflections, and draw their own faces, paying attention to the shape of faces, eyes, nose and lips, and to skin, eye and hair colouring. They should write their names on the back of the drawings. The next day, hold up the finished portraits and try to identify them.

☀ Geography/Maths

- Ask the children to create make-believe maps of King Belvedere's kingdom on squared paper. They can draw the palace, the grounds and the surrounding countryside, and landmarks such as rivers, lakes, mountains and woods. Write grid references along the top and sides. Ask the children to use the grid references to make up questions and instructions for their classmates, eg, 'What's in square 3B?' 'Draw a fountain in 6D.'

☀ Literacy/Art and Design

- Talk about healthy snacks. Ask the children to choose one healthy snack each, and design a poster with a slogan that will encourage others to try it, eg, 'CARROTS AREN'T JUST GOOD FOR RABBITS!' Display the posters around the dining hall.

Stage Plans

◦ PRECIOUS TO ME ◦

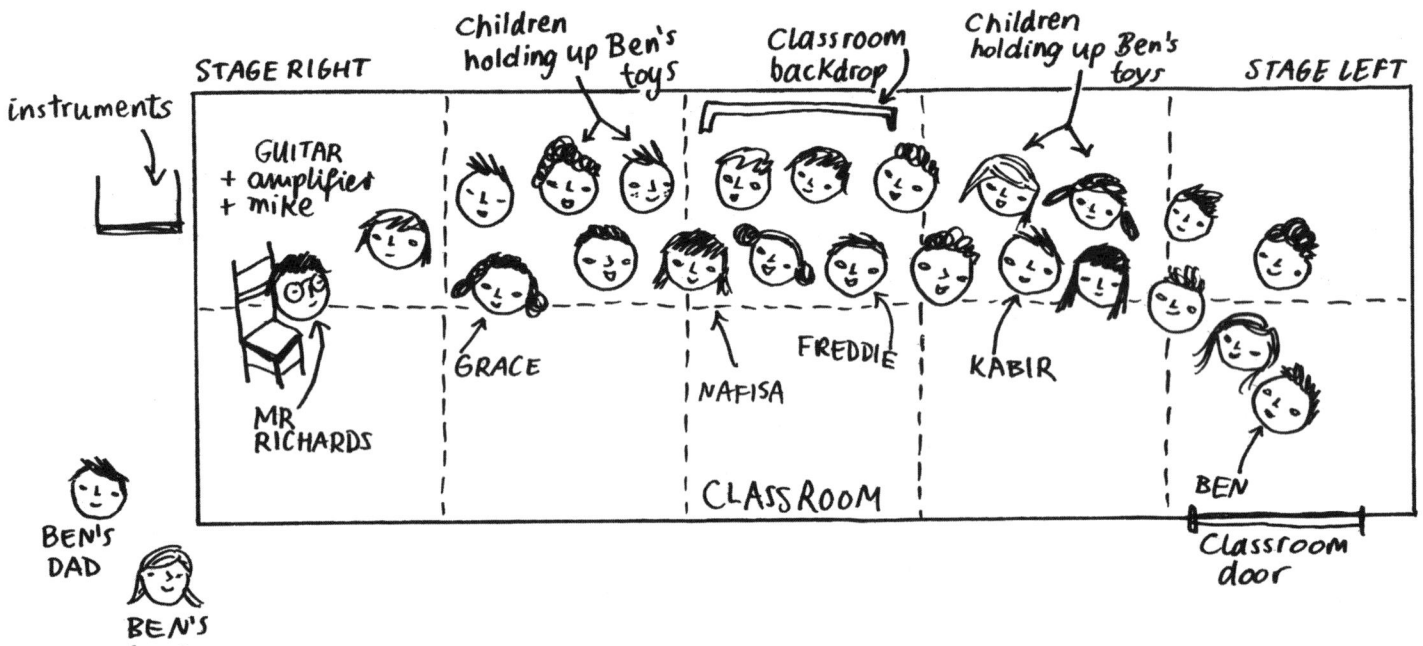

Tiddalik

MONSTER Ps AND Qs

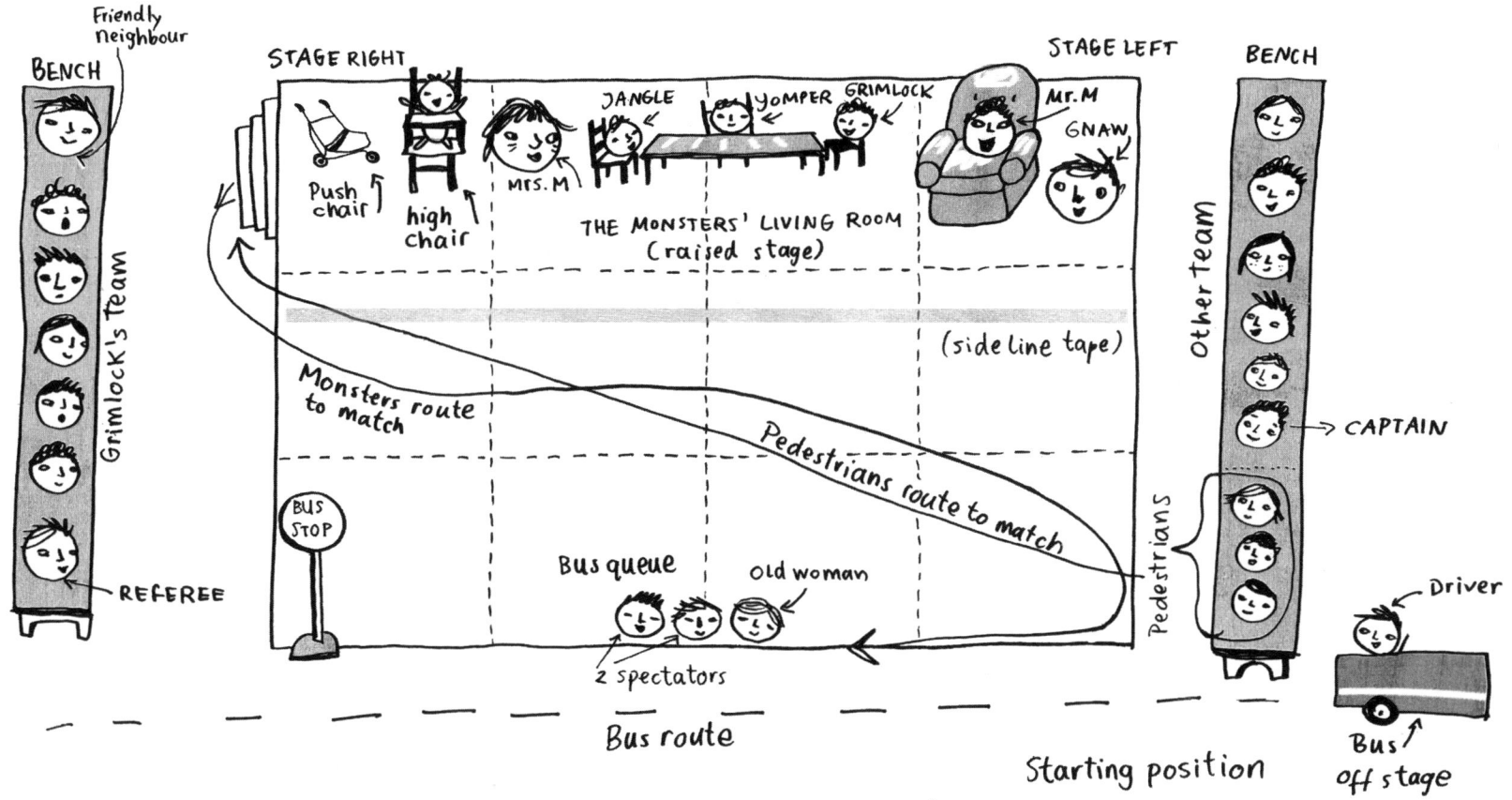

BENCH

Friendly neighbour

STAGE RIGHT

STAGE LEFT

BENCH

Push chair

high chair

Mrs. M

JANGLE

YOMPER GRIMLOCK

Mr. M

GNAW

THE MONSTERS' LIVING ROOM (raised stage)

Grimlock's Team

Other team

(side line tape)

Monsters route to match

Pedestrians route to match

CAPTAIN

REFEREE

BUS STOP

Bus queue

Old woman

Pedestrians

Driver

2 spectators

Bus route

Starting position

Bus off stage

MONSTER Ps AND Qs

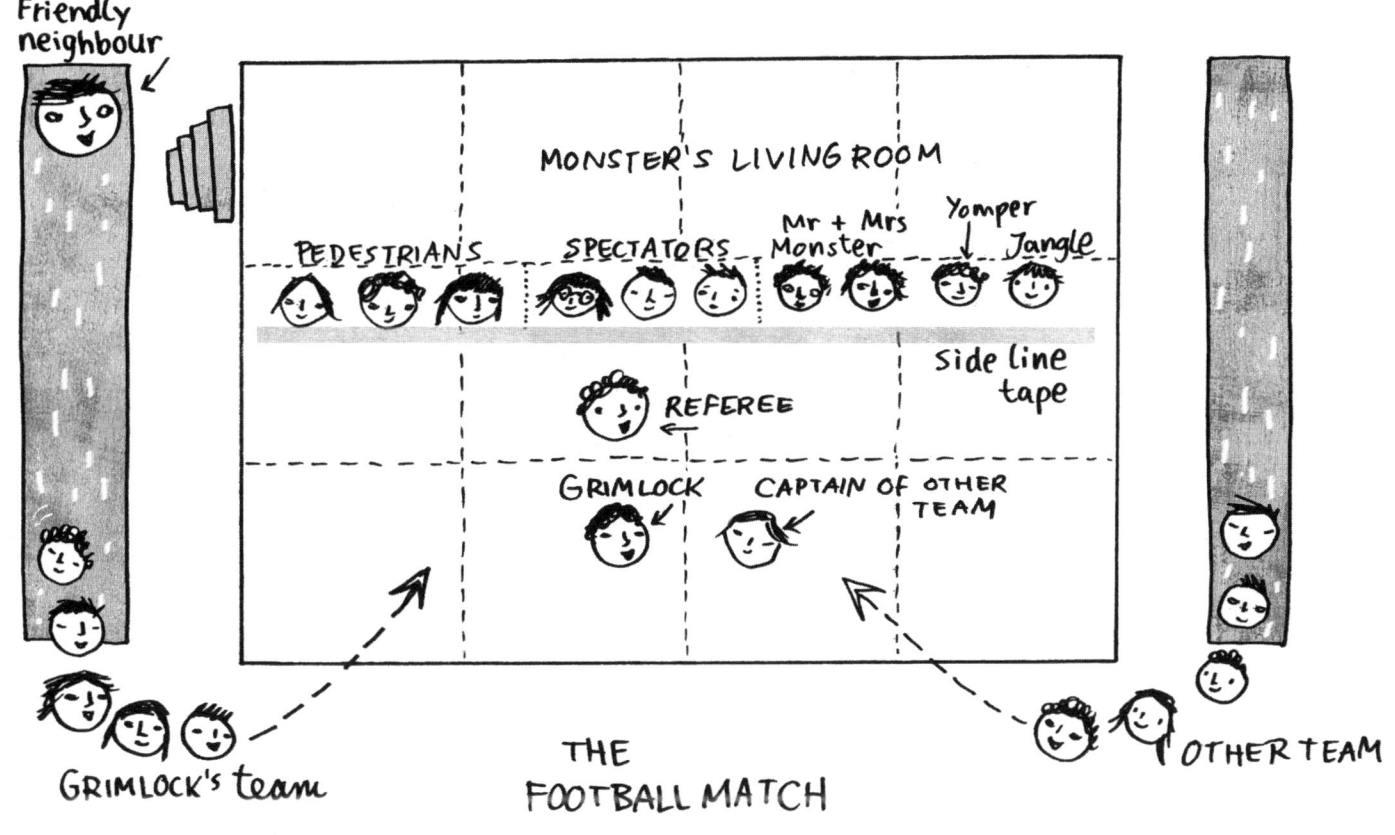

Friendly neighbour

MONSTER'S LIVING ROOM

PEDESTRIANS

SPECTATORS

Mr + Mrs Monster

Yomper

Jangle

Side line tape

REFEREE

GRIMLOCK

CAPTAIN OF OTHER TEAM

GRIMLOCK's team

OTHER TEAM

THE FOOTBALL MATCH

MIRROR of TRUTH

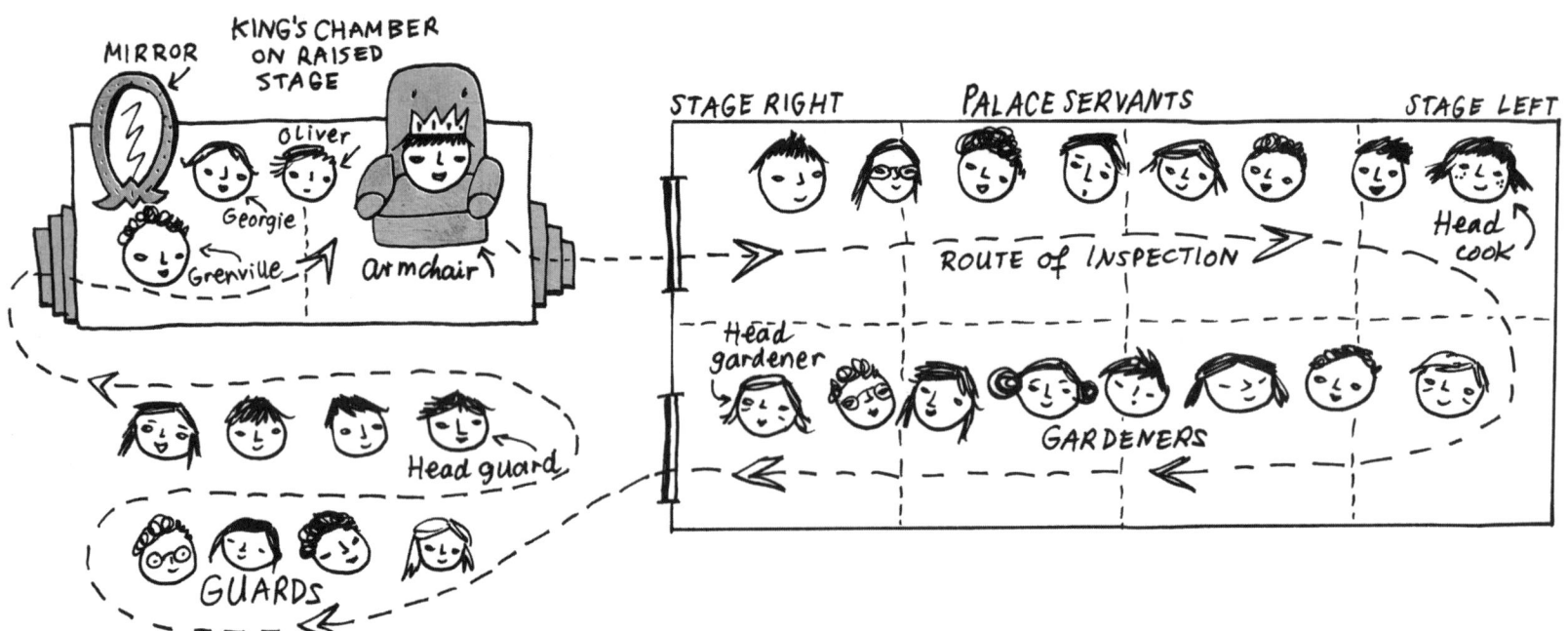

MIRROR

KING'S CHAMBER ON RAISED STAGE

Oliver

Georgie

Grenville

armchair

Head guard

GUARDS

STAGE RIGHT

PALACE SERVANTS

STAGE LEFT

ROUTE OF INSPECTION

Head cook

Head gardener

GARDENERS

SEAL Links

☀ Precious to me

Relationships
I can tell when I love or care for someone.
Ben knew he loved his little sister and wasn't afraid to let everyone in his class know it.
I can share people I care about.
Ben and his parents shared his baby sister with the whole class.
I can talk about my feelings when … I have to share someone … that is important to me.
Ben explained to his teacher and classmate why he was so fond of his little sister.

Getting on and falling out
I know that people don't always see things in the same way.
Ben and his classmates were able to see at first hand that people valued their possessions for different reasons.

☀ Tiddalik

Getting on and falling out
I know that people don't always see things in the same way.
Tiddalik was very selfish and didn't think twice about drinking up all the water. His animal friends, however, thought very differently.
I can see things from someone else's point of view.
In the end, Tiddalik was able to appreciate his friends' point of view concerning sharing the water.
I can use my ability to see things from the other point of view to make a conflict situation better.
Eel realised that Tiddalik was becoming distressed by the aggression being shown towards him, and found a solution that helped to diffuse the situation.
I know that sometimes anger builds up and that I can be overwhelmed by my feelings.
Four animals got very angry with Tiddalik and wanted to hurt him.
I can decide with my group about how well we have worked together.
At the end of the play, the animals could see for themselves that by working together, they had managed to achieve the outcome they wanted.

Going for goals

I can say what I want to happen when there is a problem (set a goal).

The animals knew what to do to make Tiddalik release the water in his tummy.

Monster Ps and Qs

New beginnings

I can sometimes tell if other people are feeling sad or scared and I know how to make them feel better.

Grimlock was sensitive to others – he didn't like seeing the pedestrians being knocked over by his mum and stayed behind to pick them up and apologise.

I know that I belong to a community.

Grimlock (and his teacher) knew that politeness helps people to live together in harmony.

I know what I have to do to make the classroom and school a safe and fair place for everyone, and that it is not OK for other people to make it unsafe or unfair.

Grimlock (and eventually the rest of the family) appreciated that being rude to people in the community creates bad feelings and unhappiness.

I can help to make the class a safe and fair place.

Grimlock did his best to make his friends, neighbours and fellow citizens feel secure.

I can help to make my class a good place to learn.

Pupils who apply Grimlock's policy of being courteous help to create a good learning environment.

Getting on and falling out

I know that people don't always see things in the same way.

Grimlock was in a difficult position because his family thought it was OK to be impolite.

I can see things from someone else's point of view.

Grimlock rejected his parents' views because he knew that rudeness can make people feel unhappy.

I can use my ability to see things from the other point of view to make a conflict situation better.

Grimlock set his family a good example and, helped by other people the Monsters encountered on that day, managed to persuade his parents and siblings to change their behaviour.

☼ The Mirror of Truth

Good to be me
I can change my behaviour if I stop and think about it.
King Belvedere had got into bad habits. Without the encouragement of his three loyal and caring assistants, he would probably never had made the effort to change to a healthier lifestyle.

Changes
I can tell you what a habit is and know that it is hard to change one.
King Belvedere had got into bad habits. He changed them because he was motivated and enjoyed his new regime.
I know that I can make choices about my behaviour.
By the end of the play, King Belvedere understood that in future, he could decide for himself how he would live and what the consequences would be.

Going for goals
I can choose a realistic goal.
The assistants chose an ambitious goal on behalf of the king. Its success depended on the king really wanting to find the Mirror of Truth. As is happened, the assistants knew the king well, as he rose to their challenge, even though he didn't realise what their actual goal was.
I can break a goal down into small steps.
The assistants, on behalf of the king, broke their goal of getting the king back into good health into manageable steps.
I can tell you what I have learned.
The king eventually discovered the trick the assistants had played on him, but he reacted by laughing, indicating that he approved of what his assistants had done, and had learnt his lesson.
I can tell you why things have been successful.
The king knew why he had become a fitter and healthier man, although at the time he wasn't aware of what was happening.

Melody Lines

Precious to Me

I wonder

The world is full of won-ders and de-lights,_____ Like friends and pets and

toys and fros-ty nights._____ But if I had to choose some-thing

pre-cious to me, I won-der what that spe-cial thing would be._____

Holidays

Ho-li-days___ are pre-cious times, When ev-'ry-thing___ feels good and new.

Blue skies___ and spe-cial treats, Laugh-ter and friend-ships too.

Let our music come alive

One, two, three, four, five, Let our mu - sic come a - live.

Six, se - ven, eight, nine, ten, Hit those joy - ful notes a - gain.

Wibble wobble

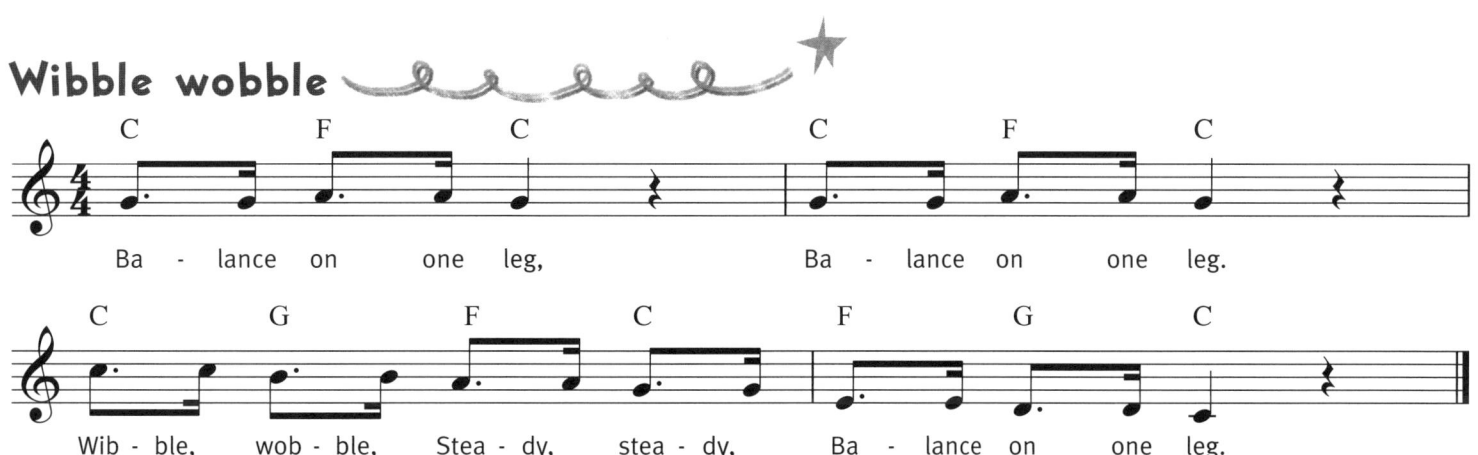

Ba - lance on one leg, Ba - lance on one leg.

Wib - ble, wob - ble, Stea - dy, stea - dy, Ba - lance on one leg.

Tiddalik

Thirsty

Par - don me do if I have a moan, My mouth's as dry as a din - go's bone, This

thirst is the worst that I've ev - er known,__ Tid - da - lik is thirst - y!

Wa - ter! I am gasp - ing! Wa - ter! Throat is rasp - ing!

Wa - ter! Must have wa - ter, Tid - da - lik is thirst - y!

No! No!

Don't be a mean - y, Tid - da - lik,__ Don't play such a nas - ty trick,__ That's so snea - ky,

that's so chee - ky, Don't drink all the wa - ter! No, no, don't you think it!

No, no, don't you drink it! Wa - ter's there for all to share, So don't drink all the wa - ter!

Melody Lines – TIDDALIK

Let's all pull funny faces

Let's all pull fun - ny fac - es, Let's be sil - ly and daft.___ The last time we pulled fun - ny fac - es, Ev - 'ry - one laughed and laughed. Let's all pull fun - ny fac - es, It makes you gig - gle and grin.___ It's ea - si - ly done, it's lots of fun! And ev - 'ry - one can join in.

Laughter wins the day

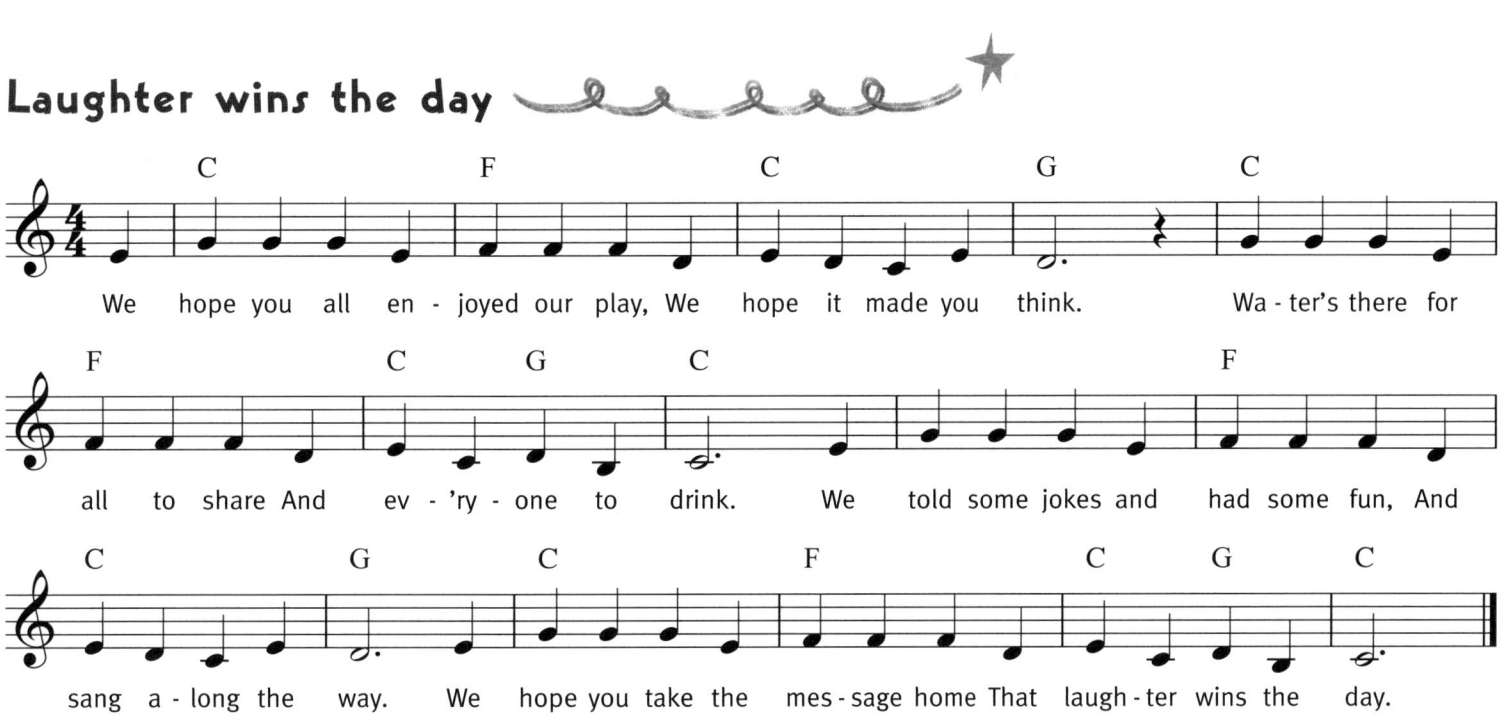

We hope you all en - joyed our play, We hope it made you think. Wa - ter's there for all to share And ev - 'ry - one to drink. We told some jokes and had some fun, And sang a - long the way. We hope you take the mes - sage home That laugh - ter wins the day.

Monster Ps and Qs

We don't say thank you

We don't say 'THANK YOU' and we don't say 'PLEASE', We
They don't say 'THANK YOU' and they don't say 'PLEASE', They

don't say 'AF - TER YOU'.___ We nev - er, ev - er say 'I'M
don't say 'AF - TER YOU'.___ They nev - er, ev - er say 'I'M

SOR - RY', 'HEL - LO' or 'HOW D'YOU DO?'___
SOR - RY', 'HEL - LO' or 'HOW D'YOU DO?'___

Coutsey is catching

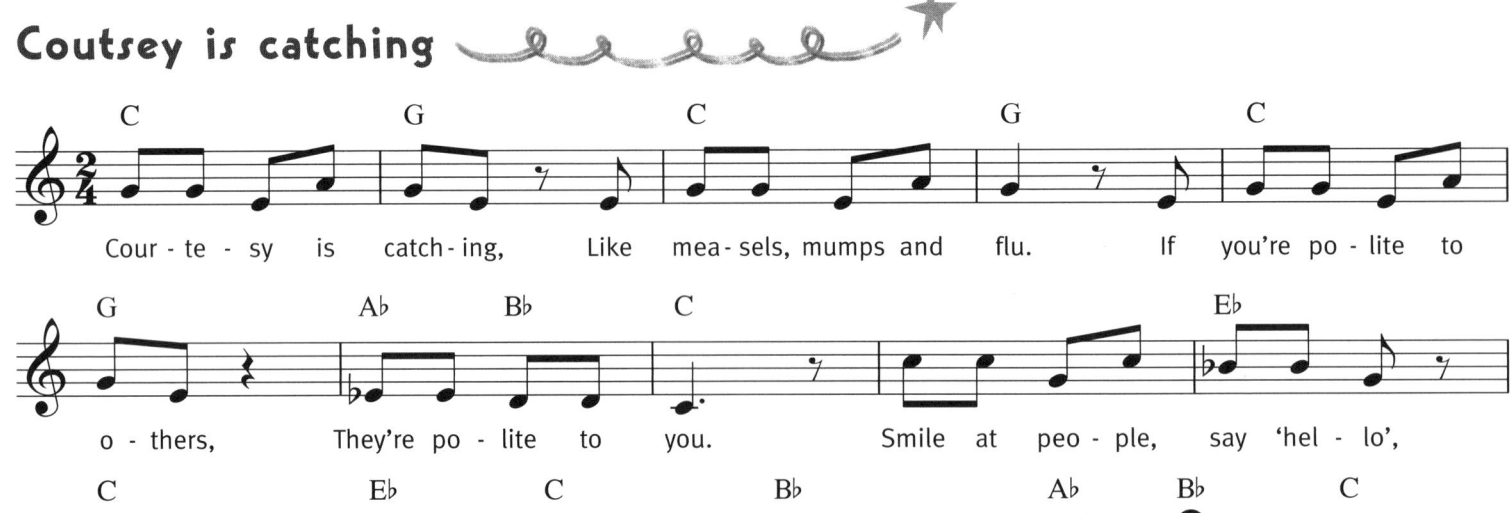

Cour - te - sy is catch - ing, Like mea - sels, mumps and flu. If you're po - lite to

o - thers, They're po - lite to you. Smile at peo - ple, say 'hel - lo',

Mind your Ps and Qs. O - pen doors, show you care, Po - lite or rude, you choose.

Melody Lines – MONSTER PS AND QS

We do say thank you

	F							
We	do	say	'THANK	YOU'	and	we	do	say	'PLEASE',	We
They	do	say	'THANK	YOU'	and	they	do	say	'PLEASE',	They

	C				
do	say	'AF - TER	YOU'.____	We	al - ways	say	'I'M
do	say	'AF - TER	YOU'.____	They	al - ways	say	'I'M

		F	
SOR - RY',	'HEL - LO'	or	'HOW D'YOU DO?'____
SOR - RY',	'HEL - LO'	or	'HOW D'YOU DO?'____

The Mirror of Truth

Searching

| F | Dm | Bb | C |

(1) In and out the boots and hel - mets, In and out the boots and hel - mets,
(2) In and out the halls and kit - chens, In and out the halls and kit - chens,
(3) In and out the trees and foun - tains, In and out the trees and foun - tains,

| F | Dm | Bb | C | F |

In and out the boots and hel - mets, Search - ing for a mir - ror.
In and out the halls and kit - chens, Search - ing for a mir - ror.
In and out the trees and foun - tains, Search - ing for a mir - ror.

Where's the mirror?

| F | | Bb | F |

Search - ing here and search - ing there, Where's the mir - ror? Where oh where?

| | Bb | F |

Up and down and round a - bout, If you find it, give a shout.

Melody Lines – THE MIRROR OF TRUTH

Fit and healthy

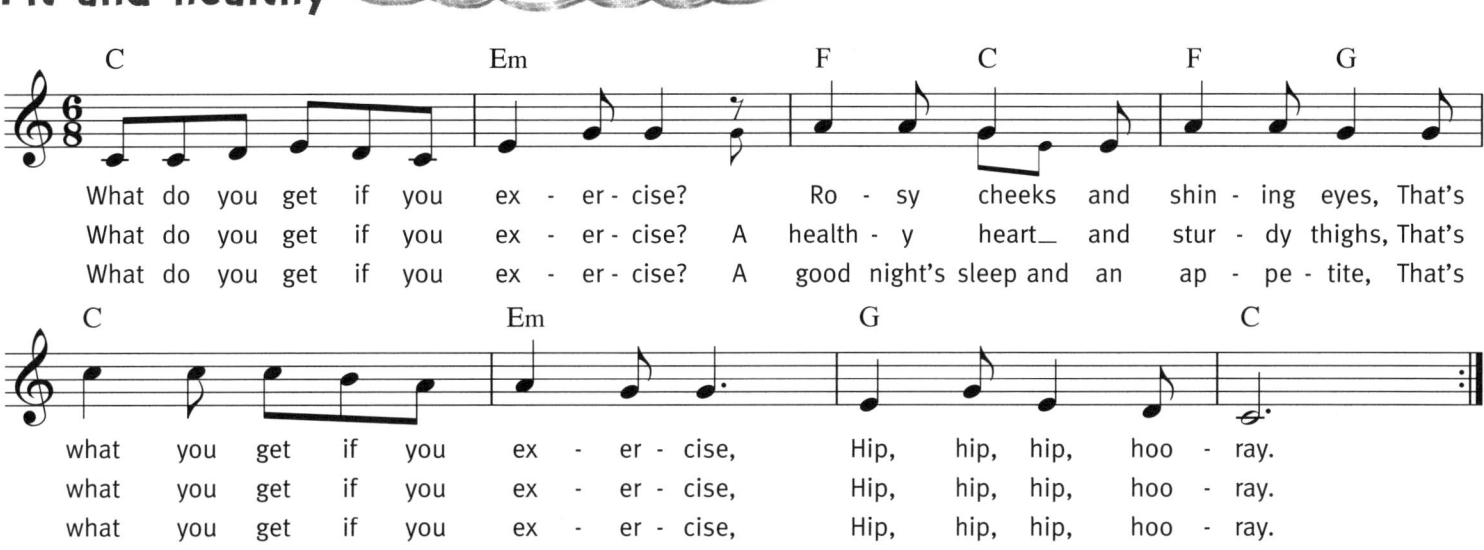

C	Em	F	C

What do you get if you ex - er - cise? Ro - sy cheeks and shin - ing eyes, That's
What do you get if you ex - er - cise? A health - y heart_ and stur - dy thighs, That's
What do you get if you ex - er - cise? A good night's sleep and an ap - pe - tite, That's

| C | Em | G | C |

what you get if you ex - er - cise, Hip, hip, hip, hoo - ray.
what you get if you ex - er - cise, Hip, hip, hip, hoo - ray.
what you get if you ex - er - cise, Hip, hip, hip, hoo - ray.

And finally ...

Performance licence information

To present an informal performance of any of the class assemblies from this publication, you do not need to purchase a separate performance licence. An informal performance is a performance, with or without an audience, that takes place within an educational establishment or church, where box office takings are less than £250.

You may also make copies of the audio CD solely for the purpose of preparing for and aiding an informal performance within the establishment for which the original script was purchased without paying a further fee. Any copies made must not be distributed outside of the establishment for which the original script was purchased, and must be destroyed once the performance has taken place. Any other copying is strictly prohibited.

If you wish to video or record a performance, either for your own internal use or in order to sell copies to parents, you must write to us separately to obtain permission. See below for our contact details.

If you wish to present a performance of any of the class assemblies from this publication where any box office takings will exceed £250, you must contact us for permission and an appropriate performance licence:

The Copyright Manager
Music Department
A&C Black Publishers Ltd
36 Soho Square
London W1D 3QY
music@acblack.com

About the authors

Veronica Clark is author of *High Low Dolly Pepper* (A&C Black), the Christmas musical *The Raggedy King* (Starshine Music), and co-author of *Three Little Nativities* and *Three Little Celebrations* (A&C Black). She was music advisor to BBC WATCH programme, *The Song Catcher*, and is a former primary headteacher and specialist in music education for pre-school and infant children. She believes that involving young children in musicals provides them with an exciting and relevant educational experience, which encourages them to experience all areas of the curriculum.

Kaye Umansky taught for fourteen years in London primary schools, specialising in drama and music. She has been a full-time children's author for the last twenty-five years and has written many plays, music books and novels, including the *Pongwiffy* series (Bloomsbury), *Three Tapping Teddies*, *Three Singing Pigs*, *Three Rocking Crocs*, and the award-winning *Three Rapping Rats* (A&C Black), and is also co-author of *Three Little Nativities* and *Three Little Celebrations* (A&C Black). She lives in London with her husband, daughter and two cats.

Jenny McLachlan is an Advanced Skills English teacher who works in East Sussex. She has written stories for children and teenagers and has created a wide range of English teaching resources. Through her work, she is involved in educational research and promoting good teaching practice in primary and secondary schools. She has a passion for children's literature and a belief that it is through engaging with imaginative writing that children learn about their world.

Acknowledgements

Story of *Precious to Me* © 2010 Jenny McLachlan
Songs: *Let our music come alive* and *Wibble wobble*, words © Jenny McLachlan, music traditional
I wonder and *Holidays*, words © Jenny McLachlan, music © Veronica Clark
Story of *Tiddalik* © 2010 Kaye Umansky
Songs: *Thirsty* and *No! No!*, words © Kaye Umansky, music traditional
Let's all pull funny faces and *Laughter wins the day*, words and music © Kaye Umansky
Story of *Monster Ps and Qs* © 2010 Veronica Clark
Songs: *We don't say thank you* and *We do say thank you*, words © Veronica Clark, music traditional
Courtesy is catching, words and music © Veronica Clark
Story of *The Mirror of Truth* © 2010 Veronica Clark
Songs: *Searching* and *Where's the mirror*, words © Veronica Clark, music traditional.
Fit and healthy, words and music © Veronica Clark

Teaching activities © 2010 Veronica Clark

Cover illustration © 2010 Tim Hopgood
Cover design by Jane Tetzlaff and Sara Oiestad
Inside illustrations © 2010 Christiane Engel
Edited by Lucy Mitchell
Text design by Fiona Grant
Music setting by Jeanne Roberts
Recorded arrangements, incidental music, sound engineering and mastering by Matthew Moore
Songs sung by Kaz Simmons

The publishers and authors would like to thank the following people:
Pashley Down Infants School
Year 2: Fran Vogels and Michelle Stewart, and children in Robins, Woodpeckers and Owls.
Shinewater County Primary
Moira Smith-Nicholls.

First published 2010
A&C Black
36 Soho Square, London W1D 3QY
© 2010 A&C Black
ISBN: 978-1-4081-2457-4
Printed in Great Britain by Caligraving Ltd, Thetford, Norfolk

This book is produced using paper that is made from wood grown in managed, sustainable forests. It is natural, renewable and recyclable. The logging and manufacturing processes conform to the environmental regulations of the country of origin.